DANGED BLACK THING

EUGEN BACON

APEX BOOK COMPANY | LEXINGTON KY

ISBN (softcover) 978-1-955765-11-4

ISBN (ebook) 978-1-955765-14-5

"A Visit in Whitechapel" was first published in *London Centric* by NewCon Press, October 2020

"Danged Black Thing" was first published in *Jagged Edge of Otherwhen* by Interbac, July 2012

"De Turtle o' Hades" was first published in *Jagged Edge of Otherwhen* by Interbac, July 2012

"Forgetting Toolern" (previously "Honey Gone Sour") was first published in *Meniscus*, April 2017

"Rain Doesn't Fall on One Roof" (previously "A Migrant Story") was first published in *The Blue Nib*, April 2020

"Still She Visits" was first published in *Unsung Stories*, May 2020

"The Widow's Rooster" was first published in *Tricksters Treats *3: The Seven Deadly Sins* by A Things in the Well, October 2018

"When the Water Stops" was first published in *The Magazine of Fantasy & Science Fiction*, May/June 2021

"Unlimited Data" was first published in *Cyberfunk Anthology* by MVMedia LLC, February 2021

"The Failing Name" was first published in *Fantasy Magazine*, August 2021

Collaborations

(permissions obtained to include in the collection)

Visit us online at https://www.apexbookcompany.com.

PRAISE FOR DANGED BLACK THING

"Seventeen genre-bending stories from Bacon (*Mage of Fools*) come together to form a masterful, Afrofuturist exploration of gender, class, race, and belonging."

—Publishers Weekly (Starred Review)

"This sharp collection of Afro-Surrealist work takes the reader to near-future dystopic states where the body and tech and magic are all intertwined, twisted, and pulled from the earth. Myths are born and undone from the quotidian and later broken down through a candid and unafraid voice."

—Ana Hurtado, judge, OTHERWISE AWARD

"Brilliant, erudite, playful…"

—LEE KOFMAN, award-winning author of *Split* and *Imperfect*

"The stories within *Danged Black Thing* build worlds that can transmute to provocative dystopias in a matter of a sentence."

– FOREWORD REVIEWS

"With the lyricism of Toni Morrison and the world-building of Ken Liu, Bacon secures herself as an important voice in Australian genre fiction. *Danged Black Thing* is the feminist science fiction debut that brings women and Blackness to the forefront."

—BOOKS+PUBLISHING

"Eugen Bacon is an exhilarating writer. Her work is daring, fierce, visceral and sensual, fast paced and packed with action, earthed yet given to flights of fancy. It is driven by empathy for the eccentric and marginalised, a simmering anger at injustice and inequality, and a deep concern for the big questions…"

—ARNOLD ZABLE, award-winning writer, novelist, and human rights activist

"The African Australian author's creative inspirations are just as free flowing, from myth to folklore to speculative fiction and Afrofuturism."

—THE BIG ISSUE

"Eugen Bacon gives us a cornucopia of dark fruitfulness. Her writing is equal parts fecund earth and fine-cut jewels; her stories juxtapose the scarred and abused with the powerfully magical, the numinous and the deceptively mundane. They travel the known world, remaking all its parts as they go, and they pull new worlds, fully formed, from Bacon's unfettered imagination."

—MARGO LANAGAN, internationally acclaimed writer of novels and short stories

"For readers who enjoy inspecting the underlayers of flamboyant life, *Danged Black Thing* proves a rich mine of storytelling prowess. Things are what they are— until they are not."

—AUREALIS

"Equal parts fecund earth and fine-cut jewels… *Danged Black Thing* is a tour de force of fictions within fictions and a rare treat—poetic, fantastical and pungent with characters of many pasts, presents and futures."

—TEXT JOURNAL

"Bacon's writing is so assured, so deliberate, so interesting—reading it, you'd be forgiven for mistaking this book for one by a best-selling international author with decades of publishing under their belt and a large editorial machine behind them. Kudos to the author for forging her own path and maintaining such high standards…"

—THE AUSTRALIAN

"Few writers in Australia are as prolific as Eugen Bacon, or as polymorphous."

—SYDNEY MORNING HERALD / THE AGE

"Eugen Bacon is a critical voice in Australian literature, one that probes and prods, questions and enlightens. She is an extraordinary poet, and while *Danged Black Thing* is a collection of short stories, the poet's voice shines throughout."

—BACKSTORY JOURNAL

SIMBIYU AND THE NAMELESS

THE COLOR is full of shade and smells like crusts of fruit. Crushed guavas, warm wet clay—that's the sweetness and mushiness about the forest. A tepidness too. And then there's a whiff of soured yam, unwashed body. Something old sniffling in the shadows.

Eyes pore over your hollow within, ticking, ticking with your heartbeat. But the hollow is dead cassava dry—all surface and dust. What sound will fall when you press your ear to its longing? Perhaps nuances of self-reflection beckoning the moon's return.

You are eighteen months old.

A crunch of tires, then squeals of children tumbling out of a foreign car. Your mother owns sandals but likes to walk barefoot. This is how she greets Aunt Prim, who is layered in batiks and swirling in a smell of flowers. She's approaching the boma under the blaze of an orange sun. Your cousins, Tatu and Saba, are giggling, whispering, nudging each other.

"Abana banu! These children!" Aunt Prim is all sharpness. Sharp eyes, sharp nose, sharp ears. "I heard what you said!"

She grabs a stick from the ground, makes to chase your cousins, but platform shoes don't take her far. Her tongue clicks. Her stick waves from the distance. Aunt Prim is nothing like you know. Because your mother is pillow-soft, her voice tender like the feathers of a baby bird. She's hooked you on her arm, your fat legs astride her waist. Her sweet brown eyes, her dancing dimples. She smells of sugar bananas —small and thin-skinned—on her chest where you rest your head.

"Sissy Prim. What do you bring us from the city?"

"Flour, sugar, and these two urchins. Look at them."

"Doing what?"

"Mischief. Can't you see?"

"Don't run it up. They are young. See how you make them hush like spirits."

"Evil ones."

Silence, then a scatter of feet. Titters spilling everywhere, as your cousins stampede around the hut in a shroud of dust.

"I swear!" says Aunt Prim. "Weye! Useless as mud."

Your cousins still running.

"Tatu!" She's the older one. "Wait 'til I catch you!"

"And then what?" asks your mother.

"She'll see."

"Don't fall on the child with a hammer."

"Mphyo!"

Your world is small yet familiar, framed in textures and shapes. Sometimes you see darkness and lizards, cats nudging and gliding between grown-up legs. You touch what you know. Listen to what you don't, but still touch it. Trust or instinct are not your diplomacy. It's all about repetition, endurance. Curiosity and hunger etched in your living.

"Tatu!" Your mother locates the cousin behind the fat waist of a mango tree. "Take Simbiyu."

"I don't want to."

"Because why?"

"It's hours of boring."

"Rubbish. Come on then, quick. Your mother won't eat you."

"But she might!"

You whimper a little as your mother loosens you from her hold as she presses you onto Tatu's back. "Saba, go inside. Fetch me a wrap."

He runs.

She rubs banana smash off your face with spit and a thumb. She takes the floral wrap from Saba, secures you on Tatu's small back. "Now off you go. Stay away from the river. Be children. Be alive."

"Like a drum?" quips Tatu, kicking off her shoes.

You gurgle your glee and bop on your cousin's back. Her naked feet race away from the homestead, past a few huts, some goats and grumbling chickens, and into the tree line.

"Wait for me!" cries Saba.

It's an uneasy sanctuary for play. But Tatu has chosen it. She zips into the forest full of spidered twines and shiny leaves—green and swollen like avocados, but they smell of the watching dead.

"I don't want to go there," says Saba, stalling his feet.

"Iwe! Don't be a coward. Just come!" Tatu loops through the trees. She doesn't care that Saba has chosen to run back home. She unknots you, plants you against a slanted candelabra tree and its bad milk. A perch of white-backed vultures with sharp beaks are on the tree overlooking the river with its whitewash where you'll likely die—not from the water's malice that is of a different kind, but from a bask of crocodiles burrowed in its mud and blinking to darkness.

The river is changing. You know this without knowing how, or why. Tatu doesn't notice. She's poking in the mud, digging for crabs. A black octopus climbs from the water's surface. A mist that whispers a name. You understand it. You're one with it, bopping your anticipation.

They find Tatu's husk, and you—crawling and full of play around her shrivel, babbling a name.

You are four.

Tumbling down the village with your little friend Uhuru from the hut next door. He's your companion now. Your mother is distant, busy with farming: yams, sweet potatoes, and tomatoes to sell at her stall in the market.

You feel the shift in the air before you see it, before Uhuru's squeal.

Silence is a dog rooted on the ground, no heart behind it. Smell is a non-event whose jaw is wide open, eyes glassed in shock. It's the maggots that carry an answer—slipping in and out of intestines torn from the dog's belly. Worms coiling, uncoiling, negotiating with the corpse, draping around each other in a sepia slime of focus.

Uhuru sees the dead dog and its maggots, but you see more. He's unaware of the fragment—something broken—and it has chosen you. That something is the shade of a tree, a lurching darkness assembling, disassembling. A menace approaching, human, nonhuman, waving tentacles.

It's the octopus from the river. A shadow jerking and crawling like the maggots but with a story, and there you are. Your mouth is moving in silence, unfolding words that are a breath in a messy language full of space. And you're ready and available, full of history and a future, just unwilling to once more hear the name.

"Run!"

As if Uhuru needs encouragement.

You are five.

You don't remember much of what happened—it was a blackout. They say you were sitting at the edge of the forest, all giddy and merry inside the circle of a serpent's coil in broad daylight, mumbling a name.

The creature was lethargic, a swell in its belly. Village men pulled you out of the circle—only then did you cry like someone was ripping off your limbs. But the rock python was too lazy to move. They sliced out broken bones and what was left of Uhuru.

It changed how people saw you. Now, they whispered.

At first, they poured holy water and crossed themselves when you passed. In time, they forgot what you didn't.

You are seven.

You know how to mingle, but it's not a school day. You like the sweet and mushy forest near the river. It's cooler on the skin here. Oranges and purples in the bright green foliage, flowers drooping, sky-craning, leaning into you as you walk by.

The rogue sisal belongs near the candelabra tree but today it is here. Chorused trilling, squeaking birds. You adore nature in its glory. Look, a shrub, weather-trimmed to resemble the bum of a gorilla facing away. The *chwee chweee* of a cousin bird hushes with the cough of a giant bird flapping its wings above the broad star-face of wild cassava leaves. The sound of water running. You can smell it: wet soil and reed.

No one is here, just the birds and you. You forget tussles with harmless children who sometimes tease, and you all but hold back from calling up a name. You're nothing like them, the village tots like Juzi or Vipi or Bongo—never curious about the skull of a dead zebra, the neck of a fallen giraffe. You discovered them at the edge of the forest. You once saw a leopard drag away a child. People are afraid of this wilderness, not you. You've told no one about the cave and its dripping of warmish water near the shores of the murky river hiding crocs and snakes.

Today you're here where it's dry but cooler on the skin, the name of an entity in your head. But it won't come.

You are nine.

You are more and more in your head, but perhaps it's your mother's guilt or penance that farms you out to Aunt Prim. Your mother walks you miles and miles from the village and your river, from dawn to noon, until you reach a market. There, she haggles about the price of a ticket and puts you on a bus.

"Your aunt will be there when you reach."

"But I'm hungry."

"Eat the oranges and casava in the handkerchief I gave you."

The bus pulls into a town station at dusk.

Aunt Prim is there, all right, layered in batik, swirling in a scent of leopard orchids and kudu lilies.

Slap!

"But I didn't do anything." Your hand on your cheek.

"That will put it right out of your mind to do anything," she snaps and hauls you to her car.

"Where's Saba?"

"Boarding school, like you should be."

You look at her. You don't have to say the name in your head because you feel it. The octopus mist is swirling, swirling inside. All this way … how did it come?

That night Aunt Prim wakes up to lizards crawling in and out of her hair, up and down her body. She sees a yellow-eyed cat sitting on the sill of her bedroom window, in the blackness looking at her.

The incident creates the grim reality of your tacit agreement with your aunt to be civil to each other. You do your chores, do your school, where students and teachers give you no mind, and you prefer it that way: left alone, except on the football field. Aunt Prim lets you be, and you let her be. Sometimes she gives you Saba's comic books: *The Adventures of Tintin*.

In this world, you run up tides and variations by intuiting. Your entity is here, a specter that enfolds you when you close your eyes until you reach the edge of reason. In life's lessons, will your sixth sense do you solid? Or will it dot your portrait of purpose, all obscure?

Right now, you don't know. Each day is a swaying floor that smells of city, sea, and trap. You should be angry, fatigued from it: who's scripting your part?

A dream with a name is your handhold.

You are thirteen.

A scout spots you playing football in a stadium. You're clean with the ball, hitting the scoreboard. The other team is wide, nowhere near. Your own team is a shocker, but you're the most valuable player.

The scout is leaning against a post, scribbling notes on a sheet held in a clipboard.

A blackbird with an orange beak hops on your path, vanishes into air.

A name that is peril and chance slams like a door in your head.

You are fifteen when they clear you for travel. Your scholarship has come through. Aunt Prim is still wary but today all teeth, a wad of money tucked between her breasts.

"Get settled there and send for your cousin Saba. You'll make us proud."

Does "us" include your mother? You haven't seen her in years. Sometimes, you wonder about her, then forget. You lost your mother the day Tatu died. She stopped breastfeeding you that same evening, and her touch hardened.

"Jump in my car. I'll drive you to the airport," says Aunt Prim.

"I'll take a taxi."

The road to the airport is full of potholes. The foreign contractor used cheap tarmac, and someone put a lot of money in their pocket. It's midnight when you pull along the kerb to the International swing doors. "Keep the change," you tell the driver. The scout and the people he represents are either very generous or keen to have you. You step out of the cab and further from all you know. It's a story for no tabloid, only you are listening to its tale. You understand all you've lost forever, yet it's the answer for right now.

You arrive at the checkpoint without phoning your shoeless mother who may be waiting for your midnight news. For the first time, you understand both dying and torment, and the yawning schism of passing over.

You're sullen all the way to Melbourne Tullamarine Airport.

Six a.m. A queue of people at customs. A thumb sucker catches your eye, barks his cry into his blonde mother's shoulder. Perhaps she's an expat. She's wearing a t-shirt that says: *African drumming: be alive.* It reminds you of Tatu.

The uniform's face when you reach him is a stop sign. He demands papers, gives you a look that says you don't have them. But you have them. There's no ambiguity in your compliance. Still, he enters a dangerous discussion.

"Empty your pockets." It's full of notes—jottings that remind you where to draw the line. "Your phone," he says.

"Enough," you say.

He starts to bark orders, but the smell of dead bones has a point. It also has a name. Alarms are beeping like mad. The uniform's mouth is opening and closing, like that of a fish out of water. His skin is losing luster, in fact graying. Restraint, for you, will come with age. Today is a life behind you, and a fuckwit between you and the life ahead.

Your ride is a big white van with a sign: A hive of bees? A sack of guavas? Goget.com. The man driving it is not the scout. He's a scruffy white man with ash on his head and a back-turned cap. You saw enough tatty whites in the planes and the airports, stopovers in Dubai and Sydney, but attributed it to a lack of flying etiquette. Now here's another one who held up a sign to retrieve you at Arrivals. A sign that said: *Simba Yo*.

You tap him on the shoulder. "That's not how you say my name."

He grunts.

He's not a man of many words. He drives along the labyrinth of the metropolis. You reach the college campus, and he throws your swollen suitcase off the van.

You're not sure whether to tip him. You pull a note, mindless of its value, and offer it.

"Nah. Keep your money, mate. We don't do that in Melbourne." He reverses the van, drives away.

You report at the main office arranged with phones and computers. It has pale walls and high ceilings. Glistened trophies and framed certificates stare at you. The girl behind the desk is a topaz-eyed nymph with burnt-orange hair.

"You're early. Semester starts in a week."

You sign forms. She gives you a student card, keys to your room, an entrance fob, and a map. "Not many students around, but you might bump into the odd teacher."

You drag your suitcase into the gray monolith that's your dormitory.

Later, you'll take a walk to acquaint yourself with this new world full of cars and shops, and houses built like wedding cakes; you saw a tiered one when Aunt Prim's friend got married. You'll discover a restaurant that serves wok-fried prawns with lemongrass, curry leaf, and shrimp. You'll wash the food down with water, not a glass of white.

On your way back, you'll go past a young woman with a face swallowed in sunnies, dragging a leash and Tintin's dog. She'll take one look at you and remember to remotely lock her car.

You connect early, though you don't know how to read her, the new one. She comes at you on campus, peering through a camera. She lowers the lens. Big gold eyes shimmering on her face.

"Yer 'ave a look like a man on a mission ter forget a past."

"I'm not sure," you say.

"Then yor name's Tipsy."

"It's whatever you like."

"Just messin' wiv yer. They call me Mali." She extends a lingering hand that fits in your clasp. She's attractive: full lips on a triangle face. Hesitant smile. Hair so black it's blue, braided in rows and tails on her head.

"I wasn't expecting that accent from a black girl."

"I'm not sayin' anyfink about yor accent." You look at her, amused. "I'm bloody well British. Media and Studio Design. Are yer also on a scholarship then, guv?"

She's wearing a sunflower flow, bohemian in style. It waves with the wings of a butterfly. She's a twist in your story now—your gut tells you this girl is important.

"I'm a lesbian," she breaks your heart.

Mali shines. The longer you know her, the shinier she gets. It's not just the gold in her eyes—sometimes she's splashed in a beam of light from the sun.

She introduces you to grilled hunky dory and deep-fried chips. You miss chicken hearts and gizzards, slowly stewed in a pot on a three-hearth stone. Simmered with four sprigs of coriander and natural pink salt from the flamingo lake.

You take Economics. The lecturer is easy on your requirements for tasks and assignments. What matters is the field. The coach teaches you to play a different kind of football that uses hands and feet. They call it footy. The game has marks: players climbing others in leaps to catch the ball. It has boundary throws. The coach makes you a forward, not a ruckman—you're athletic but don't have the height, even though you can fly.

First match, first quarter, you're a showcase: three goals on the spot. The octopus is in you everywhere, your hands and legs fully tentacled. Bounce, bounce, kick. On the field, like this, you're one with the team. Inside kick, handball pass. Clean disposals, no waste to the dying seconds. Off-field, you're solo. Not counting Mali.

You are seventeen.

But today is its own narrative. The octopus is asleep.

Before you fall, the ball has legs and accuracy—for the other team. The field is yellow with night lights. Shadows and smells: sweat and feet. The other team's players are everywhere. The match is a brawl, short shorts as you fight. Shoulders and chests bulldoze you to the ground. Knees and shins find tiny gaps to the post. The other team's star player has a left foot that's a mongrel. Nothing you do bangs the ball on your end.

Your coach is filthy about this, his hands and mouth severe. But your body is wrong, your kick a real mess. Your skin is ill-fitting—that's why you fall.

What you want to remember is the name in your head that stands you up. The name that comes when your mind connects with a memory and latches on to it. It makes you right, just so. The name that's a voice and a ghost and a storm all at once. The name that makes you slippery through the forward half as the other team gains meters and besieges you. The name that fuses the ground and the sky like a clash of heavens and hells on your shoulders. It's a release that floats your ball long and deep and the match is changed.

What the devil? It's great. Now you understand that the entity is not always harming, it's gifting too.

You are eighteen.

You celebrate with a trip on a leased car. A three-hour drive via the CityLink to the Hume Highway that merges onto the Northern Highway. Two hundred and thirty kilometers to Echuca.

"Blimey, right, I forgot the camera."

Mali—the lesbian friend you can't read—is all eyes and dimples that remind of your mother, yet not. She's the one driving, she has a license.

Two years now, she's been giving the right vibes that could be wrong. She has slowly hijacked your life in a romance that will never take.

From when you first saw her, even as the campus grounds spilled with students—red ones, pink ones, olive ones—Mali and her cloaking of light are spottable anywhere. You find it refreshing to be around black skin, though she speaks funny and insists on pointing her lens at moving targets: birds, cars, people, you, mostly you. Saying, wow, wow, as if she sees something you don't.

Her photos of you are up close. A soldier's crop. Big square face. Thick black brows that are better less. A wide nose. A gobbling mouth —she caught you in a yawn. You wonder what she sees in you. Still, you can't read her. She holds away from more. Or is it you holding away, unsure if she just really likes you, or is bi?

"As I were sayin', Simbiyu, me pops. He'd been married, wot —thrice?"

You look at her and see sparkles. She's shimmering.

"I never knew my father," you say. "Spoils of war."

"Scars, right, yer mean, isit?"

"Too good at reading me." You're thinking: Shouldn't she be the one?

"Yer make it sound terrifyin'."

You're in trackies, but the rented four-sitter is all shiny inside, gears and buttons. She glides, purring all the way down a lone country road, the sun bearing down, a scorch in your throat.

You were once a child with a lacking story, and now worry about what's too far gone for sadness or anger. But you already determine that what *should be* is a slaughtered treat. Nothing will resurrect the impossible. Work is never cut out for you. All you can do *now* is comfort yourself under the looming moon's unreadable gaze.

Mali drives long and north towards a country town with paddle steamers on the Murray River. The evening sun is a watercolor on the horizon. Clouds frown malcontent into meantime lands. Echuca is a ghost town. You're too late for the paddle steamer, and everywhere is closed. Look, what's this: a pub named Parfitt. It's yet unpatroned but spilling with brash country music.

Please, no dogs, says a sign on the wall behind the service counter. But all you see is a memory far too big, a walking contradiction to nowhere stories. The pub with its fading décor is not the kind you pictured. A float of feathers lavishes fusty walls, but there's a hook for a coat. The man at the bar is wearing a sweater. He has eyes that could be your lost father's, his arms folded, legs akimbo. Box face, swirly curls all gray, the nose of a prince—all haughty like. He's built like a fridge but there's heat in his dislike. His eyes come and go to the sign on the wall, then at you.

You look around. There are no dogs, just you.

Mali is sparkling. "That says a bit. Like a bit."

You don't need to summon the name. You and the river octopus are one. Your head falls back, your tentacles spreading within, without. Your eyes close, your feet off the ground. Your eyes open to blinding light. You blink. All is changed. Fat toads are hopping on the counter, sliming the floor. Hundreds of lizards knocking glasses in slow-motion hours going without protocol. The man at the bar is making a noise that's a groan inside a croak. A toad is lodged down his throat. His legs have the shakes. He's deflating inside his sweater, a man-sized doll losing air. The desiccation in his skin ... The shrivel of hair on his scalp. Centuries consume him. You look at your hands—you're a shadow. Your mouth is moving in silence, your body lurching in darkness.

A voice inside the bright light says, "Me word. I don't 'ave me fuckin' camera, init? I knew yer were special."

You step back into yourself on solid ground, but your head is swirling. Suddenly you feel alone, and alone is not so fun anymore.

"Simbiyu." Mali's luminescence is reaching, your name is a caress on her lips.

As you wonder when she met her Cthulhu, she offers her lingering hand. You hesitate, then take it. She snatches you out of the pub and drives across a railway, past its station to a place you'll lean into each other, chest to shin, heads touching. Waiting—for what?

You'll spend the night at a family motel with wi-fi and free parking.

You are twenty-three.

Your team has been in the 'top four' years in a row: twice grand finalists and two cups to show for it. You are the most medaled player, constantly making headlines. You wear twice-shined moccasins. You own three cars and a tiered wedding-cake house on Summer Street in a leafy suburb.

You pay for Saba's tuition—he's family. *Wema hauozi,* says the adage. True: generosity never rots. You send money home to Aunt Prim and have built a storied house for your mother—what's family? She still walks barefoot, they say. You put electricity and tap water in the village. They finally cordon it from the wilderness when two elephants go rogue.

There's a sweetness in your bedroom, a mushiness in the air. A tepidness too. It doesn't matter when crushed guavas and warm wet clay show up, or when a whiff carrying ghosts of soured yam dumps itself with a scratch on your chin.

A crack of lightning and the devil himself plods from twilight. Then he's you, and you're offside in your leap from the bed. You land knees and knuckles on the ground. Your skin heals and takes you back to yourself and your bed. The devil smiles and wets his parched throat from a brook as you lie awake counting words and dreams sprouting from a future that insists it knows what's best before sunrise.

You look at Mali, blanketed in silver light. Glittering in deep sleep beside you.

You remember with longing your once pillow-soft mother. Her sweet brown eyes and dancing dimples. Her voice, tender as the feathers of a baby bird.

You finally understand the nameless. And the darkness that rose from the river those many years ago—how it chose you. Because it's also you.

THE WATER RUNNER

THEIR SEX gave the unit a sweet musty odor like a ripened durian fruit. Zawadi lay with Mapesa a moment on the thin bed in her one-roomer, separated from the other tenants in the government complex by a box-pleat curtain she'd wrangled from a mtumba second-hand bundle. A baby was crying—groaning, more like it. Later, she stood outside in a blast of crimson desert sand, softer on her skin at dawn.

She felt thirsty and imagined cold, clean water washing down her throat. She thought of New Dodoma, the world out yonder that promised the sizzle of a shower like rain from a sleek chrome head in an en suite full of blinking marble and blond rustic wood.

She leant against the wall, tightened her dust scarf, and pictured rubbing the milk of shea butter on her elbow. It was extraordinary, beautiful that world, a place you got beer with a haircut. There, streets had names like Miriam Makeba Road, Fela Kuti Drive, Kidjo Avenue, Masekela Lane. Towers steepled to the sky, esplanades and water everywhere.

But in this beforehand, inside Old Dodoma, she had decisions to make—and the conclusions came along with judgements and mitigating circumstances that were too reckless to leave to chance.

Technology had improved on most things except housing, the climate, and scarcity of water. She rubbed on the jasmine dry wash that came with moisturizer. She licked the powder that fumigated her mouth, eradicated from her tongue the taste of sleep and Mapesa.

She looked at the curtain—Mapesa's idea. "Tenants equal more credits," he'd said, not long after they moved in together.

"Dear one," she said now, as he dressed into his cli-suit for work. "Let me know how you go."

"Easy," he said, the gold in his youthful eyes dancing. He flashed his suave smile, the one that softened her knees.

She followed the pings. Each ping came with coordinates. She bluetoothed her hoverboard—silent, solar-powered—and off she surfed.

Each day began with aplomb before worrying itself to nothingness.

By close of day, her kinetic energy was in a stupor, the hoverboard her only answer as it followed homeward coordinates to Lyumbu.

Today's first caller was crouched in a hut in Malimbili, tucked northeast of Old Dodoma. The woman was too broken to weep, but her face was already long before the grief. She reminded Zawadi of her own mother's lingering face in Nkulungu those many years ago. A sweet-looking face lean like that of an antelope. But this here hut was nothing like the fresh-smelling one that housed pomegranates, coconuts, figs, and nectarines that Zawadi's mother sold at the market. This hut in Malimbili smelled like a sewer clogged with feces.

The woman stretched out a tiny bundle. She unwrapped from it a puffed face with pupil-free eyes unshut in death, a tiny gray mouth set in a straight line. The mother had covered the child in a temperature wrap to keep it cool, unreasoning that the corpse was beyond feeling.

"What happened?" asked Zawadi.

"She's only a tiny one," the woman said.

Zawadi pulled out her device, logged the job. "Everything doesn't start with *No*."

"You'll take her?" The woman spoke in murmurs. Her chitenge—a flowing wrap—kept falling off her shoulder to reveal a leaking breast.

"That milk will sell. I can arrange for collection until you dry." She looked squarely at the woman. "It just means more credits for you—and that one." She nodded at the dust-covered boy peering from behind the chitenge. His hair was a rust color, his belly swollen. "Let him have a tug, it will help his kwashiorkor."

"The gods give. Why quarrel with them when they choose to take?" said the woman.

"You may have your own idioms, but this is not karma. If I had a word with the gods, we'd talk about why they are full of cruelty."

The woman signed with a finger on the pad.

"Instant credits when the shuttle comes to collect," said Zawadi.

She jumped back onto her cosmic hoverboard, its Milky Way whiteness a shimmer in her eyes. She soared under a red sky, no clouds. The day was yet another sizzler, you'd think the body would get used to it. Even with the government-issued cli-suit and its self-regulating system that adjusted to the environment, she never got cool enough. The suit's purpose was endurance, not comfort.

Stuck on a traffic island, she wondered how Mapesa was faring. He hadn't called. Like her, he worked in government. He was a groomer. He dry-washed old people. Took orders on ping like her; biochemicals and a hand-held hoover did the rest.

They met three years ago at a government conference in Makulu Oysterbay. It was a forum on water planning, where they served bite-size sandwiches pregnant with cream cheese, smoked salmon, and hardboiled eggs. Uniformed waiters strutted with trays holding flutes of real, clean water. When Zawadi saw Mapesa, she was drawn by the kink in his curls, then the gold in his eyes when he turned to look at her with a crooked smile from his tall frame. Wowza! A professional development opportunity that came along with dividends. It was a matter of minutes before the dividends reached her. She smelled the vanilla and wood aroma of him long before he brushed her arm. She looked at him squarely and demanded, "What's your position on the Great Leader?"

He nearly failed. "I used to think he was a fockwit, but now …"

She swirled to leave. "Clearly I was mistaken about you —"

But his palm hooked her elbow, and he cut her words with the right answer. "Only a fool tests the deepness of a river with both feet." Indeed, the Great Leader was nothing but a nincompoop. He'd already taken a sixteen-year-old as his fifth wife.

Zawadi was not done with the examination. She sneaked Mapesa to a side room at the end of a corridor. It turned out to be where they stored robot vacuums that twitched and blinked their beady eyes—not in puzzlement, more as if they understood conspiracy. There, inside the storeroom, Mapesa passed the chemistry test. She thought for days how mind-blowing his kiss, the intimacy of their tongue wrestle, how her lips trembled with new longing when he was gone.

After they hooked up, she liked the way he spined her, as she chose to call it—a run of lean, long fingers down her naked back. Aiyaiya, it gave her electricity. She loved how he spooned her, their bodies a glove fit. He told her stories of New Dodoma—it had real schools with human teachers, not robots. Students who wore emblemed blazers and went to assembly. He told her of streets where music started on cue and led you to a salt spray from a humping sea swollen with luminescent fish.

Their sex was *good*. He knew her sweet spot. He touched her and her buttocks went tight, heat and chill all over her body, pulsing between her legs, moments before the release that flowed everywhere.

But when they started arguing and he acted all snobby, she began to question his words when they met, and wondered if his reference to the fool who tested the river with both feet was not to the Great Leader, but to Zawadi.

The lights turned.

The job in Area C was a suicide: what made a father of seven kill himself? Everything. In this world that paid in credits that dissolved in a grueling economy—everything. One simply lost faith. Even though he was outwardly perfect, rigor-mortised in a fetal curl of dying agony, she had to say no. The man had swallowed rust remover. His water was compromised.

The next job was in Ipagala. It was a hit-and-run. A collision with another hoverboard. Zawadi studied the broken body—the splatter of what was left at the site of the incident. This fresh, the cadaver wasn't yet releasing the putrescine odor of rot catalyzed by heat.

Unlike the first mother, this one with a pockmarked face was roaring her grief, tearing hair as bystanders consoled her. Zawadi logged the job, but there wasn't much liquid. Her manager Amadeus was not going to like this. 'We're not Mother Teresa,' she imagined his disdain. 'You have no power over what's not yours.'

She couldn't log the murder in Chang'ombe but made the appearance of inspecting the body, the collapse in the matted head where the skull had fractured. The caved cavity released a creamy ooze onto the naked floor. The girl had whiplash and lacerations on the arms and legs. Blood still seeped from her nose.

"This is a matter for the police," Zawadi said. "Call me when the body is cleared."

She finished before lunch on a burn in Uzunguni. It was a wealthy neighborhood—neat rows of identical thermal-controlled bungalows inside a fenced complex. The houses were built of phase change material that absorbed latent heat and gave cooling. Housewives drew leisurely strolls with robot poodles on manicured lawns.

Zawadi walked along a garden speckled with the pink blush of peonies, the yellow stretch of leopard orchids with reddish-brown rosettes, the milky dash of impala lilies gilded in red velvet, the snowy blossom of baby's breath. But the flowers and their ultra-sheen were all fakes that would never wilt. Here, there was no lingering of nosy neighbors like you might find in the cheaper suburbs. Shades, paints, and glazes—you couldn't see a thing until you stepped across the threshold.

Inside one of the bungalows, a gas burner had exploded. She looked at the cooked skin peeling off the woman's body, her chin, and neck like melted plastic, clusters of charcoal on her torso. But the burn had sealed her water—Zawadi logged the job. The husband would get good credits.

Her head hurt, so did her muscles. Day in, day out, body after body. How much longer could she do this? Back in the office in Chamwino, she let herself into the shoebox that housed two desks and a TV on the second floor of a warehouse that manufactured nutrition pills. It was an embedded warehouse, a concrete and timber hybrid buried in the ground like most corporate buildings in Old Dodoma—built to stay cold as a stone church.

Her boss Amadeus had gone missing. The two of them ran the water business, coordinated with body collectors, factories, reservoirs, and the banks. But it was only a matter of time before robots took over. They were everywhere. Robots diagnosed patients in pop-up clinics and printed prescriptions from their mouths. Robots tutored children who weren't home-schooled by parents and ran online modules for those who were. Robots ran walk-in drycleaners—they swallowed dirty clothes and spewed them out ironed. They were all part of Robotix, the Great Leader's own company.

Lunch was two reds: bland pills full of protein, vitamins, minerals, water, and carbs. Zawadi swallowed them whole, grateful she could afford them, but not the water she recycled from dead people. She was still thirsty despite the nutrients in the pills. The swooning in her head told her she was tired. Yet only half the day had passed.

On days she felt extravagant, she took purple pills that came rich with magnesium, calcium, phosphorus, and potassium—this diet balanced her water, fed her skin, polished her hair and her nails, and she stayed strong on iron and selenium.

On frugal days (she and Mapesa were saving for New Dodoma), it was the grays—a carb hit that kept her brain functioning. But mostly she could stay with the blues, cheaper than the reds and just enough protein to tease the right hormones and antibodies to keep forming.

She grabbed the remote and turned on the TV to the sight of the Great Leader with his hippo head and rat brain. Nearly two decades later, he was still denying climate change. "I don't believe it," he was saying to a reporter. "It's all a hoax. Prophets of doom, that's what they are. They should be lynched."

Like he'd lynched the economy. Like he'd lynched opposition and democracy. Declared himself the Great Leader, worked with some monarch in New Russia on the secret to longevity, bought meds from New China to resuscitate his idiocy daily. It was no doubt Mapesa was a fan. And he kept harping about harvesting clinics. That the government was growing babies.

"If it's true," said Zawadi, "they're propaganda farms."

"Give the Great Leader a break. What's wrong with creating children of the state?"

"For what?"

"All you have to do is register and we're rich," said Mapesa. "I'd do it tomorrow if I was a woman."

"I'm not doing the harvester."

"Know how many credits that is? Two hundred and fifty thousand. More than ample for two one-way shuttle tickets to New Dodoma."

"Dear one," she said, 'you're good in bed. But does our talking always have to end in affray?'

She couldn't shrug the desiccated human from her last job. A woman had put her husband in a grain store for a whole year, hooked him up, skinned him, and covered him with salt like you cured the meat of a pig. The carcass was still pink—maybe it was pink-orange, but did it matter what color it was? All she remembered was how he was crusted in parts, tougher than bad leather. And the face, dear gods, the face. His water was gone. But Zawadi logged the job, slipped through some credits. Was it to keep him or eat him, and was it freedom or desperation that finally led to the ping? Everyone had a breaking point.

"Is it really true?" she asked Mapesa that night back home in Lyumbu after their reds. "The harvesting clinic?"

"Don't be stupid," he said. "Of course, it's true."

"Look who's visiting."

It was Rafi, the tenant's toddler. She poked her head below the curtains. She had big gray kitten eyes. She was smaller than her age, that was clear, still crawling on her stomach when she should be toddling. She didn't play much, was irritable in the hours that the people of Lyumbu slept. Her cry wasn't the *owh-owh* of a baby, but a slow, low cry like that of a grieving old woman: *"Owwwhhhh."* It didn't take intellect to figure the child was suffering from malnutrition. Zawadi hated to imagine the teeny bub becoming another water run.

"Hello, Snotty," she said.

But the mother, whose name was Queeny or Beany, snatched in with her stink eye, taut cornrows, and tattered chitenge. She scooped the child without a word, leaving behind her smell of the unkempt.

Zawadi couldn't put a finger to it, but the woman's husband, Jiwe, made her uneasy. There was something jiggery-pokery about him. He had the type of square face with mean eyes and a broken nose you'd pick out in a police line-up. The woman looked battered, always shouting, "Weye!" or "Acha!" to her lethargic baby who didn't need to stop doing anything.

Zawadi wondered if Jiwe was a wife-beater. She'd never heard it, but she was on the water run the whole day—who knew what the walls saw? Sometimes she called him the magician—he vanished at odd hours. He whispered into his handheld, put on his cli-suit, and was gone until dawn.

"I can't do it," Mapesa was saying. "But you can."

"And who can we ask?"

He nodded at the curtain.

"Jiwe?"

"Haven't you wondered if he was in the black market?"

"You do it," said Zawadi. "I'm sick of this arguing."

"Easy," he said, and the gold danced.

She listened to their whispers—urgency in Jiwe and Mapesa's voices as they spoke. Indeed, the night had ears. Rafi was crying that old woman groan. "*Owwwhhhh.*" Zawadi wanted to stand outside in the warmth of a shouting wind and was about to swing her legs from the sheets when the curtain moved. Mapesa slipped back into bed.

He cuddled her in a spoon, spined her until she trembled with electricity. His words breathed on her neck. "So, they have running water in New Dodoma—it splashes from a tap."

She turned. "And that is news—how?"

"They have shops where you can buy sugar, milk, bread, biscuits, even beer or soda in a can—like we read in the books, how it was long ago."

"And Jiwe told you all this?" said Zawadi. "Soon you'll tell me they have hospitals with white sheets on a bed."

"But they do! They also have restaurants. You go in and sit and dine like a royal on a five-course menu. People wait on you every day, not just in government functions. They bring you poached chicken, boneless lamb, or butternut squash balls that you chew and savor, not swallow like pills."

Zawadi had to admit she was weary of soaring over burnt soil and dry rock to collect water from dead people. She wanted to see a world with clubs and the silvery glow of streetlights. Neon signs of whatever was the rage. Back alleyways swollen with cafés on ultrawide laneways. She wanted to walk in a botanical garden with real flowers and real dogs—Rhodesian ridgebacks, big like a grown-up, sleek Azawakhs prancing like sheikhs on trimmed grass.

"How many credits does this Jiwe want from us?" She toyed with Mapesa's curls. "What do we have to give for him to hook us up with the clinic?"

"I've already paid. All you've got to do is let me take you. One week, and we're sipping lit cocktails in New Dodoma."

"A week?"

"It's called technology. The eggs are already treated. From the moment of implanting, it's an accelerated gestation."

She thought of the dead child with a puffed face in Malimbili, the suicide in Area C, the hit-and-run in Ipagala, how the mother roared her grief.

"And who'll do the water run?"

"I can talk to Amadeus. He'll give you sick leave—hundreds of casuals are waiting in a queue."

She thought of the husband, hung up like a pig. The wife's eyes turned inward as if searching for her soul. On the scale of things, harvesting didn't sound that bad. Not bad at all.

"Dear one," she said. "And how much credit will you give Amadeus to agree to all this?"

They soared on one hoverboard—Mapesa's. Zawadi wrapped herself around him as if she were made of tentacles. She sought an emotional connection, but she could well be clutching a plank. There was just his wood and vanilla smell from the antiperspirant, and his solid athletic frame.

The clinic stood behind steel gates, electrical fencing, double-security doors. Surprisingly, it had hospital beds with white sheets on them. She was the only patient, and there was one obstetrician in the ward. He was a real doctor, not a robot. Either that or he was the perfect cyborg in a human body. A seasoned man with snow hair, a knowing jaw, and eyes that told nothing.

She felt thirsty. Mapesa was hovering with a smile—not the suave one. This one was off, not reaching the gold in his eyes. It was as if he, not her, was discomfited by the whole thing. On second thought, no—the smile wasn't foolish. It was the copious one of a pauper about to get rich. At all costs. As she read and signed the paperwork, she thought of that traitor Amadeus who didn't give a hoot about Mother Teresa and would sell his employee to anybody for a few credits.

She looked up at the doctor in the room blinking with lights and thought of a city with vibrant bustle and silver rain, water in her grasp. She understood that, much as she resented Mapesa right then, that full minute, it was her dream too. She wanted to walk into a neon-lit world whose boulevards resurrected names like Salif Keita and Yvonne Chaka Chaka.

She questioned her decision to be in the clinic, but her mind came at her with ecstatic thoughts of fun parks where she bought tickets and walked into the big mouth of a giant clown, and straight into a mirror maze or a spider ride or a supernova that churned her in the sky as she squealed her glee. She knew that she should ask about where the implanted eggs came from, who fertilized them, and what happened to the babies: were they propaganda for the state, products of the Great Leader's lunacy? Suddenly it struck her, and she went cold: what if they were water harvests?

But she closed her mind from that tormenting dread that came with pondering ethics or ethos and imagined escape from a perpetual drought that ate her inside out until it became normal, but not really. She accepted that her every day as a water runner was too reckless to leave to chance and understood that there was nobody to save her, that she must bequeath herself with dragon wings to separate from this world.

She would never thirst again.

So instead of asking the questions she wanted, she searched the doctor's eyes, but they were black velvet. "Will it hurt?"

"Don't be stupid, you won't feel a thing," said Mapesa.

"We put you in a coma to keep your body activity minimal," said the doctor.

He hooked her onto a ventilator, and at once she felt heady. She panicked for a wild moment—already she was losing control over her own body. But before she could ask the doctor to pause or stop, the vapors took.

Sound fell.

Mapesa's mouth was moving and she could make out the words "I love you," or "I have you," or "I hope you …"

Did he doubt that she'd make it? Her last thoughts as her head plummeted and a jaw of blackness devoured her.

PHANTASMS OF EXISTENCE

RAW REACHED into the dishwasher with a dinner plate, and her waters broke.

It wasn't the warmth and shame of weeing on oneself. This was a welcome pop, then a trickle, finally a gush that wouldn't stop down her legs.

She knew from the ultrasound he was a boy. "Oh, oh, three legs," said the nurse. "Look at that heart, he's a strong one!"

Raw didn't mind knowing, but Sloe flipped. "For fuck's sake!"

She didn't jinx it by naming him before he saw the world—*who did that?*

But from that moment, Raw started seeing her son in broad daylight. He was brown and lashy, the softest curls on his head. He looked just as she'd imagined her baby would be, and her heart swelled.

Several months of hiccupping and slow stretching, now he was ready to meet the world. Her first thought was that he was ready to meet the world, rather than he was ready to meet her. Perhaps it was unquestionable that he was keen for his mother.

Sloe walked into the kitchen in his undies, munching crisps, in between *Seinfeld*. She hated to think of the half-eaten burgers, peeled lolly wraps, and curled chocolate foils she might find under the cushions again.

He stopped short, looked at the water on the floor, then at Raw. "That's so creative."

"I'm not cleaning, you fool."

He stared at her—legs apart, a wet patch in jean overalls that made her look like she'd gobbled two wombats, and still hunched over the dishwasher.

Finally, it clicked. "It's time?" he croaked.

"Bloody well better be."

"Oh, no!"

"It's not like we haven't been expecting it."

"Shucks. Oh, dammit."

Like always he took forever to find the car keys, let alone pull on something that would fit, and get on the road. Thankfully this time they didn't have to push the car to jump the battery or run to the nearest petrol station with a can to fill the tank.

The Alfred Hospital was off a high street, and Sloe was shit at finding parking.

"There's a P sign." Raw pointed. "I'll get out."

"I won't be a minute."

"Find me inside." She knew he'd take an hour. She'd witnessed weeks, months, then years of his forever retarding her own life.

She saw her sunlit son near the entrance to Reception. Her sweet-faced toddler with big shiny cheeks reached out to her with chubby arms.

Sloe arrived flustered and cross, long after she'd filled papers, taken the lift, and was on a bed in the maternity ward with its whites and lights, blues everywhere: security-guard blue, nurse-scrubs blue, disinfected-floor blue, emotive blue.

"What's not happening?" he said, out of breath like he'd taken a million stairs, which of course he hadn't.

"Broken waters don't mean immediate birthing," explained a nurse with a lean face, roped hair, and caramel skin.

Raw looked at her gratefully. She refrained from asking "Where are you from?" because she hated it when people asked her that. Normally she'd growl or bark her answer: "Melbourne—where do you think I'm from?" And she'd watch with satisfaction as they squirmed as if caught in an act of masturbating or staring at a weeping wart on a person's nose.

"We'll keep you overnight," the nice nurse said to Raw. "But we'll have to induce you."

Raw's son came to her that night—his big open smile directed straight into the camera of her eyes.

Still, he wasn't pushing out. Sloe had gone back home on the pretext of getting supplies, but it was really to make more mess that Raw would have to clean. With a baby. Sloe returned at noon the next day, huffing and panting, with coffee from the vending machine.

But Sloe's show of support was a knock on the door just when she needed the toilet. That was precisely the right metaphor. Think of entering with no invitation, all slips and starts in a world made of slime. He was a shape draped in cobwebs sitting on her bed straight after midnight when she really wanted to sleep. She remembered years ago how he patted a coat and asked about the best part of her day after a shitty boss's rampage and her letter of resignation that pushed past reservations, pouring in a rage across the office coffee machine that wouldn't fucking behave and ran out of fucking water, and then overflowed. Sloe's kindness was like a veiled face silhouetted around her dying, asking her to strip off her clothes and write a will so she was easier to bury.

From inside her sheets, she tooted her disdain and gulped the coffee with its misunderstandings. Nobody there but a room afloat with faces that merged into shadows promising no light at the end of a bloody long tunnel.

At her lowest ebb, as she wondered what she ever saw in Sloe, there was her son, toddling and cooing, his plump fist clutching her thumb.

The constipation was like someone had shoved a rock down her lower belly and it was pulling her gravity. She felt the boulder in all its discomfort but there was no urge to dislodge it.

"Turn over," said Pumzi, the nice nurse and her roped hair, drawing curtains around her bed. Raw didn't feel a thing with the enema. All she knew in a few minutes was that her legs weren't quick enough, that underwear was an impediment and Sloe was effin nowhere in sight. She let out a cry of bliss as she sank into the bowl and the rock fell and fell until all its pebbles were gone too.

The shower was a burst of spring.

Much as Raw took to her, what Pumzi didn't say was how induced labor was a bitch. It was not a cutting knife through a tendon; this was a grinding saw through a bone.

"Will you take an epidural?" asked the nurse.

"Shit, yeah."

Her son faced her in a big-cheeked, dark-eyed brood, sucking two fingers.

The doctor with a long needle and a catheter down Raw's spine didn't faze her too much, though first, it burnt, then stung, then nothing. She moved her arms and legs and wondered why she wasn't in a giddy haze as she thought she might be.

The anesthetic blocked her pain from the contractions, but it didn't speed the baby.

Pumzi took off the gloves, straightened Raw's gown. "Your baby is approaching, but you're not dilated enough."

"What?" grumbled Sloe, pacing around her bed. "Why?"

The doctor's turn. He pushed up his spectacles and delivered the news. "The baby's distressed."

"What?! Why?!" Sloe still going.

"I think we're looking at a cesarean," said Raw in a calm voice.

"Jesus!"

"It'll be fine," she said but worried a little about the ticked checkboxes in her medical record under family history for illness: heart disease, kidney disease, liver disease, sickle-cell anemia.

She also worried about the things she'd ticked in her profiling of Sloe right before she married him—she never looked carefully at the data.

He was different at first. She met him in August. He had an edge about him, and a job.

Vivid green eyes tinged with gold. It happened so fast. Perhaps it was the peridot that danced in his stare to make her sure he was in her story. He was the center of her universe until he became a bus tour to nowhere. His collapse wasn't immediate, but it wasn't good, whatever happened. Suddenly, he went old on her. He didn't care. It's like he let himself go.

Raw let her judgment go. She juggled jobs, tried to keep things together. Sloe binge-watched TV, a jobless turd messing her living room. "Can't you apply for something?" she asked in exasperation.

"Like random?"

"Seek.com. Jobs R Us. There are heaps of places you can start."

"I had a dirty night. Frankly, I'm a bit ginger."

"From doing what?"

"Can't sleep with all that snoring."

"I was still snoring when we married. Stop sparking for a fight, get a job."

"Who's lighting the fire?"

The marriage was complicated and pressured. She didn't know why she stayed, or how she got pregnant. Sex was a rare thing, like the once peridot in Sloe's eyes—now a brownish green, no longer precious. If he were food, he'd be coleslaw.

She was thinking all this as they wheeled her to the theatre, then as she looked at the white sheet behind which the doctor pulled at her insides. On her back, she still felt swoony. Somewhere in a distance, she heard Sloe say, "Oh. Shit."

Another voice: "What happened?"

Another voice: "Stem the blood. We're losing her."

She closed her eyes, and there he was: her son. Smiling with his big brown eyes and soft fat cheeks.

Mamma. Mamm!

She opened her eyes, but everything was a haze.

Inside her dream, or reality, she saw Sloe in silhouette yet clearly for the first time. He was pacing the ward, tummy out in his undies, and mumbling, "Jesus. Jesus." She understood she'd run out of road and onto a crumbling cliff. Even as the planet shuddered inside fog, she knew there was one thing left to do for her better world, and she needed no excuse to ease her conscience.

Someone gently pressed her palm. She turned. It was Pumzi.

"You gave us a scare."

Raw looked about the room. She was back in the ward—not the general one with its white light and blues everywhere. This was a private room. She had her own walls, not curtains.

"Where is he?" she whispered. "My boy?"

Pumzi squeezed her hand. "Raw. I'm so sorry. You have to be strong now."

She was a moonstone.

That's what Col said in the play of light that was a five-star restaurant revolving around the city. "You're exotic with that brown skin. Did you know that a moonstone is also called a lover's stone?"

Gee looked at the shimmer in his eyes that shifted when the chandelier light moved. Adularescence—that's how she felt.

He was a fair type—clearly, she had a type: height, jewel-eyed. Col was sunned, ponytailed, emeralds sparkling in his eyes.

"You're enchanting. A three-dimensional sensual and seductive aura," he said in a wooing dance that took her all the way to his bedroom. "Tonight, I want you to be my dream stone," he whispered as his hands unclasped her bra.

He used a condom because hormones made her so aggressive she couldn't keep jobs, or partners. She threw a potted baby wattle at the last one; took another heartbreak to clean up the carpet, literally: she dated the tradie who cleaned it five intense weeks before he split.

Col's sex was nothing spectacular. She'd had better. He was too keen, zero foreplay, and his condom burst. She was getting paranoid—not about HIV or syphilis, but about being pregnant. Moonstones were a symbol of fertility.

It was then that she started seeing him, her unborn son. He was honey-eyed with the fattest legs. Head cocked, doing nothing, or flashing her a toothy grin. Sometimes he reached for her with chubby hands, or he was there: tucked in her arms and pulling at her breast while honest gazelle eyes locked her in a gaze.

Being a migrant, no family near, wasn't easy. Gee was behind in rent, gas, electricity, and another straw came when her three-week beau from Tinder stopped answering her phone after the burst condom. What happened to her magic? Her multidimensional aura? She was sensitive, needed handling with care—didn't he know that about moonstones? If she had flaws, anything could be remedied. Her shimmer waned with the breakup.

Love affairs were makeshift clinics for her loneliness. They were her matt repolish that grew her intensity. Was it okay to feel not okay? Outside two-week, three-week, five-week relationships, there was the workplace torment that was a different dynamic but equally bad for her.

One boss was a chestnut-haired bitch called Anita in a government department. She was a control freak who wanted to bounce into Gee's personal life, asking intimate questions about her dates. It didn't take long to realize that Anita was sand in a wedding cake—one bite, and you curse-hopped across a color-matched reception. She stuck like a louse, promising to never let go if your blood just flowed. She was a great slab of hashtag, the kind to out you in a tweet. Gee lasted two years—it was "term" employment, on payroll, not contracting through an agency but annually renewed. She gave her notice before the third renewal, unable to take one more minute of Anita.

She knew the saying "out of the frying pan ..." The next job was exactly that. At the second interview over coffee, she thought she might get on well with the shortie GM, a fair head with sapphire eyes. She'd underestimated the yawning ego of a man without height. He was worse than a shrew. Nothing she did was right. Finally, at one performance meeting, she reminded him that she was, after all, on a six-month probation ... He took the hint.

The new job—six weeks after Col—was temping through an agency in winter. Contracting, not on payroll. They were desperate, or perhaps it was the employer they represented who was desperate. But Gee was more desperate than both combined, though it meant driving along a curvy, slopy tollway as bulldozer trucks towered over her sedan, sometimes wobbling close in heavy rain.

She was a weekend driver, barely good at parking, and this freeway or tollway mania—a crisscross of vehicles switching lanes at speed, some nosing up her bum—got her heart rate up. Worse when she saw the silhouette of her son on the CityLink. He was asleep, feet out in a pram, as trucks thundered by.

The job paid a pittance and a third of that went to the tolls. Admin costs and the agency's commission were slowly killing her. And who'd have thought a "Vanessa" would be that mean? This Vanessa was, well, a bitch on a climber. A corporate pleaser who licked exec shoes and sucked senior management dicks at her team's expense:

How's that Next Gen change management expo strategy going?

I need that TotalHealth comms plan like yesterday.

Have you organized the Staff Leadership Awards—I'm yet to see something on my desk.

We need a guest speaker for next week's town hall—accommodation and flights sorted ASAP.

She spam-called Gee after midnight about the progress of a task that entailed excruciating designs of a nonsense framework—Gee refused to answer. Vanessa said nothing of it at work the next day, was all cagey.

Gee totally understood the meaning of drowning. She was always overwhelmed, sometimes rising and falling in a dreamlike state. Every day she was fighting for her life. If it wasn't on the road, then it was back home when she stood on her balcony, floors up in an apartment building, and stared at death on the horizon. Her honey-eyed child gazed back at her in curiosity, then chuckled and crawled away in play, looking back and wanting her to follow.

Today she was overwhelmed with everything all at once. The last straw came when Vanessa bellowed over another multitask. Gee got a box and packed. Her resignation was not a *Dear beloved leader* letter: there was no letter. Gee just threw into the yawn of a box pens, lip gloss, sticky notes, Butter-Menthols, staplers, tampons, notepads, scissors, spoons, and glue.

"The hell are you doing?" asked flabbergasted Vanessa.

"Calling it time. Or, if you like, getting myself boned."

"I don't want to sack you!"

"Smother. Who would have guessed?"

And Gee was gone, out of range but not new. Rent was still overdue. Emotions and tears flowed as she drove home between trucks. One tooted and veered into her lane.

As she worried again about her late periods, there, right there on the road, was her son. Not wearing shorts, runners, and a t-shirt, but sparkling in a crimson tutu. He ran down a slope towards her, blowing a whistle down the CityLink that was now a grassy hillock.

That evening, she stood on her balcony and glared at death. For the first time, she took a step and touched the rails. She saw her baby son floating in slow-motion, running towards her from the horizon. He flew into her arms, and she embraced his smell of passionfruit and melon.

It's okay, he said and rested his curls against her cheek.

She stepped away from the balcony and into her apartment.

A job was a job, and perhaps she'd let herself go with some choices. She didn't have to put up with shit. And what do you know? She was more qualified than Anita, Vanessa, and the sapphire-eyed

GM who was a shrew—all put together. She'd find something else, but she needed to go about it smarter.

And she darned well didn't need a jewel-eyed man to polish her shimmer.

Just then cramps, and a wetness in her underwear. She understood the flood was one less thing to worry about.

UNLIMITED DATA

"MUST HAVE a smartphone," the job ad said.

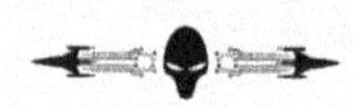

For whom does truth exist? Is it there, no matter what, or sometimes possessed by a demon? Perhaps that is why it is twisted. Untruth is straight, a racing stream thirsty for the river. Truth is curvy, a sluggish trudge filled with unease to a peak where air is thin to breathe. He looks with detachment at the lines on his palms, wonders if they are pathways to reality. But, like a slum, it's an existence with no tarmac. Escape is a memory. Just … whose?

Ping! A job alert.

He was good with gasfitting, roofing, drainage, even power outlets, ladders, testing, and repairing. Most electrical things he could do, and gardening. His hands were clever with greenscapes. He could water and feed lilies or stinkwood, trim shrubs or mow grass, fertilize sunflowers, or pluck cashews from the plant.

What he wasn't good with were lies. The employer hadn't been upfront at the interview about the data, how it was out of pocket.

When he closed his eyes, he forgot about poverty. On special occasions, he took his wife Natukunda to the village dance but now there was a toddler in tow, so they could be famous on the red dust a mere fifteen minutes, as laughter drowned out the drums before baby Mukasa rejected his temporary sitter, often an old woman, and demanded in wailful chorus his mother's breast. And the boy was greedy: he had to expose both tits before he stopped screaming.

Kaikara wished he could see it, how it was before Mukasa, but his eyes were broken, reflections of lost dreams fluttering away with locust wings. He swore he would never do it again, but fate was a tricky thing and a poor man had one solace.

Already Natukunda's bleeding had stopped and her breasts looked tender, even a little swollen. And though the toddler was still suckling, Kaikara suspected his wife was pregnant again, especially with that constipation and her craving for calcium stone, soft as chalk to chew. He reached out a hand to the gods of the mountain and demanded a better explanation.

He was an itinerant handyman on call, peddling over fields, tarmac, and potholes, moving from suburb to suburb, gasfitting, roofing, draining, mowing. *Ping!* Another job and he wheeled to it, phone in his pocket. But doing jobs on call gobbled data.

The black market was in Kabalaga. The wet mire, as he weaved around the slum and its tin roofs, walls made of carton or nylon, told him that the bunch of jobless youths with a prowl of eyes staring at his bicycle were not harmless. They wore jungle shirts and sandals made of tire.

The programmer he visited demanded a month's wage, the whole 6000 shillings of it. But even that was better than the bundle data deal of 40MB a day for mobile internet at 500 shillings, or 25MB a week for internet everywhere at 1750 shillings. That is what the employer was offering to slash from Kaikara's wages, leaving him in debt.

He looked at the programmer named Sanyu, like the radio. "Bluetooth, you say?"

Natukunda had a stall at the market in Old Kampala. Wood, sticks, and sacks held the ramshackle thing together. She sold pineapples, mangoes, watermelons, bananas, and jackfruits, sometimes papayas, guavas, sweet potatoes, and tomatoes. What she earned was a pittance. But she could buy the occasional gomesi of imported cotton, six meters of it. Rose and lime were her favorite, puffed sleeves brightly colored and reaching the floor. Each gomesi fitted her just right, its sash over her hips. When the meters allowed, she made a headdress.

Sometimes she sent money to her parents out east in Mbale. They were always sick with malaria, bilharzia, or dysentery, and the witch doctor's herbs and beheaded cockerel were not working. The old folk needed to walk into a clinic, and the white man's tablets cost money.

Now she looked at her husband as though he wore empty tins around his leg. "You're mad, foolish, or both," she said. "Take me back to my parents, and they will return your dowry."

"Crooked wood shows the best sculptor. The programmer is working with nature. His invention will change our lives."

"And who knows about this progoramy?"

"Everybody."

"So why aren't they buying it?"

"He who can't dance says the ground is full of rocks. But you and I know better than that. We dance like there is no tomorrow."

"And you say a chippy?" she said.

"Yes."

"Inside my body?"

"Yes."

"Will it hurt?"

"So tiny in your neck, you won't feel a thing."

"Like when I cut my foot on that hoe and the dokita at the clinic did me tetanus with a needo and I didn't get sick?"

"Yes, easy like a shot. You're doing this for us. For you and me and Mukasa. And your parents. I can work with no worry about data on my phone, and you can send more money to your people. It's important that you do this, Natukunda."

"For whaty?"

"Unlimited data. It's called Bluetooth. Waves from your body will connect with my smartphone and we'll pair. You'll never need a telephone for yourself—your whole body will be a smartphone. And I'll never need to buy data bundles again. It all comes with the chip."

"Bullytoothy for how long?"

"It lasts a lifetime," he said.

"And a man named after the rediyo told you this?"

"When you show the moon to a child, it sees only your finger. Natu, try and see the shiny moon beyond the finger."

"Why can't you do it?" she asked, as Mukasa whimpered drowsy-eyed at her breast. She tucked her wrap around him. "You take the chippy, Kaikara."

"A woman is the queen of the Earth. The code needs your fertile body to work properly."

Truth wakes him at night in a sense of another life. He feels below the surface, needs a hospital now. The glint in a glazed eye, what can he trust? The sound of breaking between them. Her eyes now close from his lie, a promise that ushered vultures. She's forgotten how to dance to his whisper. And all he knows is to fall. But he remembers everything.

Everyone was complicit in a fact that was neither fiction nor myth, but data. It did not depend on age or knowledge, just the insertion of a chip that started with an ideology and set into code.

The first victim was Natukunda, in her twenties. She started displaying black moods and would have battered her toddler Mukasa to death if her husband hadn't snatched away the ill-fortuned waif.

By nightfall of the same day, the woman was complaining of severe fatigue. She refused to eat or drink, even when a relative girl—a teenage daughter of a cousin of a cousin of an aunt—brought the woman her favorite plate of luwombo: cassava meal steamed in banana leaves and served in groundnut sauce.

Natukunda wouldn't consume anything all through the next day. She developed a dread to be seen and spoke in undone language, dreams inside dreams. When her husband dragged her from dark pockets under the bed, a corner of the pit latrine, under sacks in a grain store ... she came out scratching at him and tearing at her neck. But she also displayed a shortness of breath.

The woman had forgotten her name, that of her child, and her husband's.

"Natu," said the husband. "It's me, Kaikara."

She blinked at him.

By the time her eyes lolled and her body shuddered, she was sobbing through tissue, blood, and spit. It was too late to predict anything other than that her chest would stop moving. Her pulse dimmed and then vanished, and no air came out of her nose.

Just then, glass-eyed, she gave one last shudder.

Heaving words fell from her sigh and cast swirling. They formed a line like night ink and, to anyone who could read—sadly, her husband couldn't—the words in a jumble said, "Live, tracking, assessment, non-conformance, positioning, proof-of-concept, market, network usage volatile sad unmute hop on hop on hoponhoponhoponhopon nononononono."

The programmer climbed onto the roof of the penthouse in Muyenga for a full view of the moon. This suburb, famous for its hills, was the Hollywood of the diaspora. It showcased in the top ten richest neighborhoods in the world. Looking out at the horizon, he understood it was the first time he had fished in a sea of wealth swollen with ghosts of lost dreams.

On the roof, right there between scarlet dust and a galaxy of waltzing stars, he shut his eyes from tragic memories. What happened in Old Kampala was the first of anomalies.

A POD OF MERMAIDS

RAIN WAS A hungry widow. That wet August dusk, the heart talked history—Angerboda had only to check its pieces, each heavier than its size. The widow it was, each droplet keened with shoeless children, but the rain's harmonica was filled with brandy and brine.

It was a repetition loud and strong all the way to a bubbling river. She had roamed the world, Loki in her ear. What was a few minutes visiting this self-centered Earth that had no welcoming? A world that wanted its visitors to bring their own cups, cart their own plates, even haul the very doors to knock upon.

Nothing was free here—you paid for gazing at the tangerine moon that had roots in the footprints of the gods. It was here on Earth that Boda understood, really understood, grief.

Loki's betrayal! He had turned away every one of them, Angerboda's sons, including her heart of hearts, Fenrisúlfr. Who would do this? Bind his son in a magical chain of feline tread, the coo of a fugu fish, the mustache of a widow … and blame it on the boy's mother.

That's Loki for you. Same Loki with whom coupling shook stars, shot them hurtling through the skies like the seed of a god. Same one whose whispered endearments were everything and nothing. He had only to say "Boda," tanzanite and black opals in his eyes, and the touch of his gaze, his words ... diffused a nebula within her. It lit, shimmered. Even in afterglow, Angerboda shined brighter than Sirius.

Grief was missing a view of a crystal lake, not hearing hummingbirds breathing at dawn. Grief was capsizing, all weighted down when right there was a saving log.

Grief was sitting alone at a station—no chugging trains along the line, no passengers lugging cases full of maps, leaves, and dreams. Just her and the peel of paint on a bench.

Grief was the same question inside every border of a cupboard, and she was sitting knees up in its dusk.

Grief was missing things that contradicted their truth. And as the lake moved in the rhythm of a gentle heart, grief was the handwritten envelope with a blank note.

It was no wonder she fled for her life after Fenrisúlfr devoured the sun in rage. How he plotted revenge! What cunning led Loki to this, and why? Sure, he had an eye for Freya and her sorcery, her gold, her war, her death. But Boda was fine with polyamory—she had her eye on Sif, the wife of Thor, also inhabited by the oracle Sibyl, the very same oracle who finally freed Fenrisúlfr—only after he'd sunk his teeth into his arm in rabid effort to set free.

Boda thought with longing of her once palace in Asgard, the bridge across the rainbow that led to it from Earth now useless—Boda could never walk it without crossing to her death.

But now there was this Earthling boy. A mop of curls, walking, walking, sucking his thumb. He didn't look like he knew or understood grief. All he knew was his mother. That she was missing.

Boda swooped to the ground. "I am she."

I am she? Of course, she wasn't!

What was more, what was less? When the tot peered at the rivers in her eyes, and she gazed back at him, at herself through the stare of this child, who was curious more? Was she the litmus test of his world, or was he the test of hers? When she closed his hand in her gentle fist, and he let her weave her fingers into his wet and sticky clasp, who needed comfort more?

She remembered the giant kitten in Asgard, seeded from Freya's snow kitty—a vain one but so fertile—and a tomcat full of secrets; he arrived from Frigg's and Odin's household. The kitten would arch its back in a drowsy stretch after a nap under the golden arcs of the palace, weave around the paws of giant marbled lions, and deeply purr. Gazing with affection upon the sight, Boda would often wonder: who felt the rainbow more?

It had taken her centuries, and that's a long way back and forth. Time wasn't what it used to be. No longer smooth as a liar, now it was just dirty with unfinishedness. But she had found him.

The new sun was white in the sky, replenished with flames long after Fenrisúlfr had spat it. She looked at the future and saw details to a form. He was but a child. A black boy with tight curls on his head. He was the new road, the one that never was. Her body ached with possibility closer than it appeared. A mirage.

The boy spoke a different language from hers and didn't understand her answer. He asked in toddler-speak the same question twice, verbatim word for word, but all she heard was whoosh, whoosh, and a sigh of caves.

Her answer became a question and even it made no sense. He was a child of everyone, but he was hers. Surely, the sun or moon shone when it was their time. So she gave herself time. All she needed was a response—and the sigh in the distance spoke. Wait, it said.

She coasted to the horizon as she pondered, the boy getting smaller and smaller. She leant her head against snow clouds, shivering against the sky. Was it Sibyl the oracle, the whisper in the breeze, that urged Boda to bid goodbye to all she knew? It was a murmur in the boy's language: whoosh, whoosh, a sigh of caves.

Suddenly she believed in what the boy would become. It wasn't easy, but it was worth the try. She knew what she must do. She had to trick him back: Loki. She gazed again at the world below. The actions that were impossible in her world roused awake in the forest called Earth. Four times it had failed her, because ...

Because of Loki, that's what. Four times he had found her and meddled with each boy. As Boda fled Asgard—running away to what? To find goodness and hope, or to bring it to others—Sibyl showed her a glimpse of a black boy who was the future. What Boda left behind was a demented Fenrisúlfr who roared hurricanes out of Asgard and into Florida, the Gulf of Mexico, Jamaica, Cuba and Haiti, New Orleans, Guadalupe, Barbados, Martinique, and St Lucia.

Boda's heart staggered at the first boy, so tiny, so full of need. His narrow eyes sparked at her coo, "I am she." His full face, fat nose, concealed a natural meanness that Loki saw. General Idi Amin Dada of Uganda—that's who the boy became. Eight years he made history no one wanted to remember. He ate his favorite wife! They found remains of her head and her feet, styled with henna—dogs and dolphins for loyalty—in his fridge.

The second boy, small-eyed, full-lipped. A face full of contemplation. "I am she," murmured Boda, and he fell into her arms. How was she to know Loki would again interfere, make this one so paranoid he lived in a hut in an ancestral village? Hid his wealth under a straw bed. So disgusted of anyone with education, he slaughtered all those who wore spectacles. Francisco Macías Nguema of Equatorial New Guinea—that's who the boy became.

The third boy was himself bespectacled, but only Loki understood the dangerous smile on that dark skin smooth as velvet. Call it an iron fist—they were killings Boda was powerless to stop. Teodoro Obiang Nguema Mbasogo—that's who the boy became. He ate his enemies' tentacles, their brains.

The goddess knew it was time to leave. For each time she empowered, she lost. Her power waned. It took years to rebuild it. Sometimes centuries. But she flew back and forth across time. So maybe it didn't matter, but could she be eternally patient?

A mother is a mother. When she saw Félicien Kabuga—the little boy who was a Hutu, she saw need in his ebony eyes, a dependency she had never found in Fenrisúlfr. How was she to know that Loki would turn this needy-eyed child to carry out genocide? The hate that spewed from Radio Télévision Libre des Mille Collines was not enough to give warning. Machetes. Did you know that, first, they hacked at the Achilles, so the victim couldn't run? A witch, her name was Zura Karuhimbi, anointed herself with herbs and dung, and unleashed spirits on the militia. So much so they spared Boda hiding in the shrine of Nyabingi, the god of that world.

Boda understood the shining is what Loki found. It led him to locate her and each new boy. She needed to hide the gleaming. She sought the right method for no right answer. There was no rationale to it.

The elusiveness of choice came with a cascade of sensation when she saw the orphaned waif with hoofbeats in his heart, his warm breath that wielded symbols and horns in the wintry fog. Was he a wall, a bridge, a river? A unicorn? What creature was he, so able to plummet her defenses that—yet again, the heart needs what the heart wants; even immortal gods fall ill with craving—she arrowed her gaze into a silver pierce that trapped distance between the galaxy and the boy?

It was a retro axis or a fractured quadrant that unboxed pages from her past. It burst forth a picture that was out of time. A picture that was a future, never the past. It was her story and there was conflict, much conflict, and it was continuum. She was still thinking this as she swooped in a whirlwind that owned the space as part of itself.

The boy grew bigger and bigger in her sight as she descended once again from the horizon until he existed in her same quadrant. Was he a problem, or a solution? This she didn't yet know. But she took to the defining myth and spoke her prevailing belief in tangible words that were a murmuration of starlings and a sord of mallards: "I am she."

He peered through his tears, saw a fabric of the sky in the face and skin of a woman. She moved her hands and stuttered a sound, but it was all a silhouette of shape, an interpretation of form. He thought of his mother, her last hoorah, the touch on his face before she vanished.

Grabbing a coffee! she'd cracked, in that street voice of hers accustomed to harshness. Stepped across cracks into the pavement, into a 7-Eleven, and away, she became a shadow. He never saw her again. Slipped away, like the grease that was his father, lubricated to thinning, but still a tarnish, the slime of a memory. Oily breath stealing on windows at full moon. He didn't know many windows. But there was one in the sky, a woman embossed on it.

When his mother crept away, he hadn't known what to say. He'd simply walked ... until he found a bridge the color of sunned eggshells. He looked down from it and watched the toes of black rocks dipping into the murky waters, chasing the last light of day towards the city that hid his mother.

Clumps of river grass listened with him to the silent sound of wash, a giddy glide of wet tires on the tarmac's slippery surface across the road behind. He took the trail down the bridge and away from the shore to where a queue of autumn trees stood naked and gray, ghosts of twigs where leaves should be.

Memories flirted with his nothingness, the solitude of rough wet sand beneath his bare feet shuffling towards the urgency of unremembered love. It was no place for a child, rags, and bones. But it was all he had—until the sky woman came and went, and came again when she heard the yearning for a mother in his soul.

And said, "I am she."

A man in a van sweeps past a silhouette of trees. A girl in a frock stumbles on a pebble. A couple wearing beekeeping veils clasp hands around a park with hordes of yellows, reds, and greens. *Stay safe on the tan,* a sign says. A woman swoops in a cascade of wings from the gray dawn, nearly crashing another sign: *Overtake in single file. Keep 1.5m apart. Keep left.* Another sign says. A duo of Italian grayhounds in blankets—ginger on their tread, ah, winter's bite, they follow the leash. *Limit gathering to two people.*

The trill of a bell miner, the chirrup of a reed warbler. The display of a black swan on freshly mowed grass around the water conservation garden. Back a few months, who would have assumed this rage, this burn, this dread inside? Do notions start a flame? It doesn't make sense to believe it.

But it is what it is: death by a thousand cuts.

Pause, then thunder brings him home. He's hoisted in the air, suspended on power tentacles, trapped in a time warp with a goddess of the sky.

Pause, her moment in history. She's ensnared in a linger, caught in a repeat of destiny, obsessed with yet another child. It's always a child. A boy. A loner. He's her keys, her shoes.

He's unfamiliar with the arrangement, but he'll feel something before the drift of sleep. Before the storm's loud whisper releases him from the tethers of heaven's umbilical cords and rests him cold at her feet.

She's a stranger in a land of colors. Bells ring on empty streets filled with metaphors of wet and broken. Salt or glass? No applause in the revelation, it's too late to say anything. Instead, she listens to the chime of the bells until they go quiet to the caroling of magpies perched on amputated stumps. It's a sweet-throated roll and warble, complex calls marking territory. In the silence that follows she feels like a secret, a dagger from a meteorite deliberate to terminate. What would you do with all the power in the world?

Talk is what she does first. She tells him about shepherds coming home in peace. "That's how you get the milk sweet," she whispers in his dreams. He's cradled in her arms, the child of everyone. "Be a mountain," she says to him, "or lean on one." And teaches him about girls. "They are more. Girls are more." She teaches him to start living.

Just then she does her good deed and throws it into the river. Not him, her new son. She opens his mouth and blows her shining into him. He glows and glows, as mermaids grow in him, angelfish full of rainbows.

He convulses, opens his mouth, his eyes closed tight in sleep and then opened—only the whites around his irises showing. The first of the golden little things with tails glow from his foaming lips and swims.

Boda watches the merpeople fall out of her new son, tiny mermaids that swim this way and that along the Yarra River that winds its way through Greater Melbourne. Swim, swim ... in a scatter under the Bolte Bridge, Hawthorn Bridge, Hoddle Bridge, West Gate Bridge, Victoria Bridge, Seafarers Bridge.

Swim, swim ... Some will empty into Hobsons Bay. Tails glowing as they swim, all the way to Bass Strait, the Indian Ocean, the Pacific

Ocean. East to Africa. North to Asia. West to the Americas. Swim, swim … their messages of goodness and hope swallowed in gleaming. Unlimited futures to the world, they will each find a boy …

Loki will never find them all to blemish with his cunning, as Boda lives, a mortal with her son, on borrowed time.

WHEN THE WATER STOPS

As THE CLIMATE turned, it hurled at them bushfires that razed huts to the ground, dust storms that swept away families, drought—all the cattle and sheep gone, reduced to skin, then skeletons. At first, the villagers took turns on the bleed, sharing dreams and fears, understanding that as a people they were the same.

But a typical grown male has a blood volume of just five liters—a forty percent loss is deadly. The threshold thirty-nine percent has only ninety-two percent water in it; the rest is washed away in glucose, hormones, proteins, fats, vitamins, mineral salts, and carbon dioxide—what good is it? $C0_2$ may induce dizziness, tiredness, restlessness, convulsions, or coma. So, given all the minuses, how much water would be left from a bleed to go around a village?

They sifted the question in their minds while volunteers, having bled for the clan, sucked on cactus leaves and sap, figs, and desert ants for four to eight weeks afterward. But still, they were not strong enough to take another turn when it arrived. The loss was not replenished.

So where first they volunteered, now they drew sticks—it was plain luck, or missed luck. A stick was a stick, a short one was short. If you drew it, your fate was sealed, your only solace that this death would not be a lonely one, but rather a communion that met society's needs.

But even the drawing of sticks stopped eventually. It was a sacrifice too big. So now it was a matter for those with money, or bigger sticks, to determine who to massacre.

And that determined whose ashes would float in the air, figuratively speaking. What really happened took place in the vat.

The woman in the vat

What she's doing this week is sitting in a bowl, right there in the heat shimmer. She's awash with memories of drowsing, unfolding, everything in slow motion. When she looks back on this time, what will she remember? She watches the smoke swirling like a benevolent hug, giant clouds bubbling out the words: *Where are you now?* Her soul is an object brightest in the sky. Today, she's a bleed. Tomorrow is a wish.

The leader of the nation

Ten years ago, the big leader came out of his shelter, determined to occupy the steps of a shrine opened as a museum to the Pope. He stunned human rights leaders, a few high courts, and many mothers when he pushed out his lip and held up a Bible for one full minute as cameras snapped. Riot police fell with batons, rubber bullets, and gas masks on peaceful protesters brandishing slogans about the art of cherishing and love.

What was a drop of blood when the economy outweighed civil unrest and stocks soared higher? Did you see the Dow, a gain of 267 points? And the advances in the Nasdaq Composite? Evolutionary theory was all about natural selection of the form that would leave the most copies of itself.

Light-years on, every archbishop in an alternate universe, outraged by the misuse of a facility of worship, would consider the historic violation of the principles of humanity and utter three spaced words: I. Can't. Breathe.

Protests were always ugly, thought the leader. And a new election was coming up.

The rich woman in the metropolis

When the water stops, the blood must flow, says the woman with a rainbow diamond shaped into a bangle around her wrist. The billion-dollar brooch—a set with an aurora pendant—was a gift from a cousin of a cousin of a great-uncle whose name she tried to remember but couldn't. It was just too hard.

She flourishes from the catastrophe of others. Blooms on the unimportant. Like the people in her cellar, beggars from the village. Theirs is a narrative she doesn't believe in, the kind of story reflected in old photos by art historians. Her fabric is the politics that gave rise to Hitler, Mussolini, and Idi Amin Dada. She can't help it if those people don't belong in a near-perfect picture. They are mistakes, awkward memories that float a different image every time she looks, never authentic. There are many books about humanity, but this is hard!

Turn off the sound of their groaning! she snaps to her servants. The moaning is a sound that's never black or white. It doesn't obey the rules of composition. If their cry is a question, it's a cry in a language of Babel. She doesn't understand its vowels, syllables, syntax, parables, or context, and it's impossible to try. Because that's so hard!

What's not hard to understand is vintage produce with a good nose. The ones from the village come at a good price and their blood is pure, uncontaminated by the city's pollution. Village blood combines the right acidity with a sweet aroma of smoke. Bacon and pepper, violets inside a copper finish.

And vintage blood must flow for the survival of her species. She cradles with affection a labradoodle puppy to her breast.

A village husband under pressure

The revolution came when he alluded to reason.

It was a reason created from the reflection of fourteen hungry mouths and three dry cassava biscuits to go around. It was a reason that made him ask the question: wife or children? She'd brought them into existence. They initiated a cycle of living that was a torment.

Perhaps his was an excuse to be unkind, to give voice to everyday hatreds, resentments, regrets ... They crept in like dwarf monkeys and grew into pests: stealing, raiding, and all that. He was not the sort of person to hold a grudge on matters that came along with a sad marriage, so it was right to say it was fear that decided his choice.

When his wife's revolution came, there was no question where her truth lay: husband or children?

He made things happen, yeah. Sorry. They said what happened in a vat was quick.

He did miss having someone to rant to. But there was enough money to feed hungry children now, the youngest just two. Afia, the Friday-born child. Abimbola, the rich-born child but always poor. Amara, the graceful one now potbellied and bald with kwashiorkor. Chi, Ke, Re, Po, the quadruplets with nylon hair and eyes filled with sand.

He made things happen because, after the wife . . . Fourteen options still.

Afia, fifth of fourteen motherless ones

I am a broken egg on a blistered road. A dying bird on a razor-wire fence. The jackal trots this way, that way, sizing up how to eat me. My nostalgia is here again, no school, no soup. Just an empty sky whistling as we bury our dead. I am a marked card—red marks the spot. The arrow will whiz into the eye of a dried-up fountain. Are you my mother? There's a skeleton trapped in the black mamba's hissing. gray feathers swirling the wrong way.

The youngest child speaks

I'm in search of something I don't know. There's a hand and a gaze, a smile and a scent. It's a comfort, it's a warmth. I don't remember the face that comes and goes, the love that is a crack. It's complicated, it's unsafe. Blurred and full of crumble.

Nostalgia, a great-uncle with empty sacks, an odor of mothballs in his breath, his eyes a fortress against hope. You think of this moment, over and over, wishing you and the rest of the world remembered different.

A STRANGE COMMUNION

I SEEN DE DEVIL up close last Easter. He ain no beast wit horns, but de night were sure hotin up.

We was sittin on de second pew, spits away from de preacher who shooks de room an holler words like hoodoo. I gives him A for commitment. De choir blasted *He-llaelu-iahs* like de firin squad. Jus den de door near de altar bounce open an de devil hisself flowed in clean across de church, de scar of a purple leaf bobbin on his arm. Maybe his silk laugh set de tone, maybe twas his game face or jus a bit of both.

I reckons he'd take out de preacher but he ain done any of dat. He set right next to ma daddy atween Mamma and me. De devil, he spokes to ma fawk. But none of dem seen more but de parody of de preacher, hear else but de riffing of de choir.

His face pull out of his body, spokes to dem fawk but he look at me. He whisper soft as corn syrup, sweet as ice cream, yet his words carry five loaves an two fishes. He say: "Son, you wanna do it right, nose all front? You gots to lure de soul of de preacher, de uniforms, de cardinal and de POTUS right square."

He gaze intimate twas a kiss. "An when you do, get all dem souls, no Jesus bleedin crystals on de cross can raise de goddam world from ruination."

Hell!

llaelu!

iah!

MESSIER 94

(WITH ANDREW HOOK)

I WAS PASSING through an altered line-up of suspects removed from linear time, but none revealed their wind or percussion, not even a state of mind. What I needed was a shift that happened inside out, outside in, something fixated on call and response. What I needed was a zoom, possibly in never out.

Doubting the character of heavy metal and electronic dance on the face of each suspect, I meditated upon the lamentations of jazz and folk, blues and soul, improvisation, syncopation, and swing. The fingerprints of bass and horn, steady drumbeats on two and four sang my soul, choired my knots, and chorused empty buses and skeletal dogs in that shadowy place of Zacchaeus come down.

I opened my mouth and rhythmic riffs of a melodic bridge broke out with sway, ensembles of a pentatonic scale—five notes per octave in an ancient tempo. Then, only then, did I recognize that the sound was in my head, and mine wasn't a-passing through. I was there, a suspect. *The* suspect. But what was my crime? And *who* was judging me?

Here I was, looking at myself in a round mirror framed in ebony wood against white marble tiles, above a vessel sink in the shape of a mosaic bowl patterned in coral, in a bathroom that wasn't mine. I was in a hotel suite.

The face gazing back at me wore dark circles of sleep deprivation. Something drew me to the hickey on my neck. It stirred a memory of legs and sheets, entwining and hard breathing. Something firm, tender. Touch, texture, sunshine, rainbows, rain. A build-up of little pleasures, soft and warm on my lips, my tongue, my skin, my thighs, my buttocks … until the experience soared out of this world. I remembered fusion more cosmic than a nebula. Divine wings that spread around me in a fugue of music so thorough, it irradiated inward in a pressure wave that erupted. Explosion after explosion, starburst after burst, how sweet.

I trembled at the memory, my knees all butter. But the sweetness did not dissipate my guilt. Nothing further jogged my memory. What the fuck happened, and why was I standing alone and naked in a hotel bathroom?

At first, I thought the skin on the person in the mirror was black, actually a chocolate velvet. Then it went white, speckled with freckles. No, a hue of caramel. Differences, nondifferences, appearing from nowhere. The hickey on my neck was rosy, now dark truffles. The lips stayed soft and full, whichever gender, just one set lightly painted in pillow talk, then bronze, sometimes peach. The eyes vacillated between crisp emerald and deep charcoal. The hair … there was no hair. Now fragments of a man, now a woman, looked back at me, comparing notes, confusing me with someone, something.

I looked at me, studying me with coldness or curiosity across blinking glass. Fraternal twins, identical but shifting sex. Everything was fleeting, voiceless, like an online story, an alien invasion—appearing everywhere in the suburbs, slowly around the city, where the numbers were okay but it was all mechanical.

The mirror was a language in collapsing time, memos on an Earth overgrown with weeds, a random spread of flowers. Each new study of myself was a pulse ticking with tales full of questions, each a one-night fling that begot someone else's child.

I returned to the sleeping chamber in its gold, white and black décor. The king bed all tousled was obviously slept in. Pillows pummeled. A doona—disemboweled from the mattress and collapsed on the floor. Sheets twisted in once throes of dying. White stains and a musky aroma of sex assured me something had happened here. The color of stains on the carpet leading out the door under a glare of modern chandeliers—crystal, in the shape of an inverted crown—left me nonplussed. The cherry palm print on the doorjamb confirmed my fears against rigor-mortised remains of recall. Blanks everywhere but something was all too clear:

Someone, something had abandoned this room—hurt.

The fuck?

Just then a gentle knock. "Room service." A male voice.

I grabbed a towel. It was soiled—not like a witness but the instrument of hanging. I opened the door with caution, peered at the fresh face of a young Brad Pitt. His eyes were lit with mischief; blond hair dangled in a fringe across his forehead.

"Good morning, Dr X. The breakfast you ordered."

He wasn't Pitt, just a close resemblance. He stepped into my room as the crystal in the chandeliers tinkled. I blinked. A lovely girl with a tray entered deeper into the room. The linger of her Halle Berry smile was as disconcerting as the dark sweet notes of her perfume: wood and spice. She placed the tray on a marble writing desk with drawers, lifted the cloche. She was Braddess Pitt. Brad Pittess?

I caught a whiff of cinnamon, muffins freshly baked. Something burnt and nutty: coffee perhaps.

"Will that be all?" piped a voice.

I sank onto the bed, too miserable to tip the child—the child!—perhaps a teenager. Bradelina. Bradelette? Brad-petit. He wore curls on his head, a tux and a bow tie, and the big eyes of an adorable puppy. I put my head in my hands, stared at my feet as the door softly closed.

The blood on the door and the carpet was gone.

Dr X was an intriguing nom de plume, an inescapable lie. Regardless of a shifting perspective that nagged at my psyche, I had recollections —memories, education—which scrolled through my mind like a zealot through microfiche. Data, sensations, visions, dislocations formed information I knew, moments I had lived. In addition, those strong breakfast smells suggested baseline reality. While forcing a construct upon my malleable environment, I found I could operate within different parameters. I watched my fingers mutate in the process of extending, reaching for a muffin that changed shape before my eyes. My conclusion defaulted to virtual reality, yet when the muffin reached my mouth there was no sensation of falsehood. The texture was as authentic as the taste. Perhaps it was more likely any hallucinations were narcotic in nature, as opposed to an exterior simulation.

Moreover, the frisson of those sexual sensations were susurrations around me, a cocoon for an identifiable act that anchored just as much as made no(n)sense. Those twin bodies, engulfed in the heat of it, made me wonder if both were indeed me: the ultimate in online masturbatory experiences. Yet just as I couldn't touch my right elbow with my right hand, I knew I couldn't have given myself that hickey.

And damn, that muffin was good.

I thought of a galaxy, Messier 94, itself an anomaly within others of its kind. Unlike regular spiral galaxies that were a disk of gas and young stars, intersecting a large sphere of older stars, Messier 94 did not contain such older stars. Instead, a bright central structure held intense star formations that resembled a bulge forming a ring around the oval region. Those were known as pseudobulges, hosting stars that didn't orbit randomly, but rather followed paths much different from elliptical galaxies, this morphological feature contained internal dynamics dominated by rotation rather than random motions. As my head spun in a similarly suggestive fashion, I wondered if, in the same manner that humans were eventually supposed to resemble their dogs, such mimicry might also extend to the galaxies they lived within.

The absence of blood was not an absence of injury.

I observed the room and understood there were no windows. The mirror the only glass. I tucked the last crumb of muffin into the corner of my mouth with my left pinky, then walked over to the door, which wouldn't open. A locked room mystery with myself as victim, as perpetrator.

What I didn't have was a whodunnit, more a why-how-where-when-if-the-fuck-dunnit. But was it a conundrum that I wanted to solve? I tugged the velvet sheets from their tangle, crawled into the bed, cradled myself in fetal pose, and closed my eyes.

"Hello?" is the pulsing of text pushing your eyes toward the screen like the beep of a life-support machine. "A ride to your dreams" is the ticker chasing the bottom of your screen just above the taskbar, way before you touch the mouse. "Click me" is the text that stretches, coils and spits into a divination crackling to lightning that's an anomaly: forming, deforming, dislocating. "A retro to your zeal" is the telltale promise of who knows what the fog is. "Uncover your yearning" is the lust miles away yet right here, right now. "A rite to your wishful" is the test in its pattern of urgency, telling you it's time to feed. "Click me. Now" is the tempo of a tick, first in constant intervals—two breaths apart—then faster, louder, a drum machine matching the hammering of your heart.

I woke to the auburn light of a candlelit room. Without windows, I could only suppose I had slept through the day, that now it was dusk. I looked about the room—there was no hint of a watch or a clock. But something shifted in my head, and I almost cried with the joy of memory. It was slowly coming back.

The pop-up had appeared after Adelaide.

Same Adelaide who spoke in staccato about a tumbling marriage. At her most anxious her words fell out quick and sudden as if worried she might lose her breath before she released each vowel. I let her spend herself, anticipated her closing line complete with self-deprecation. "I don't know why I'm here. It's not that bad."

"When Cedric talks to your children, Martie and Bee, and yet he is addressing you, how does it make you feel?" I said.

She burst into sobs, and I let her, finding it odd to see a racehorse cry. That's what she reminded me of: a sleek horse—long-necked, chiseled, long-legged, fine-bred. Yet she was a pleaser full of self-doubt, now huddled into the loveseat with its tilt in my office, crying her need. I gave her a tissue. She blew her nose. I handed her the waste basket.

She was one of many who brought me their wretchedness, dread, and longing. I listened to their pitifulness from my Pisces-meshed chair, then unfolded my legs, leant forward, and handed them water or tissue from the multi-legged coffee table. It was glass-topped, all branched in black and whitewash, something wild yet sophisticated.

A blend of Italian and Brazilian that made me think of an exotic dancer full of class.

Perhaps it was the wildness of the coffee table and the restraint of the heritage bookshelf, conveniently placed against the wall and facing them, not the plushness of the loveseat, that encouraged my clients to wail, giggle or roar their ineptitudes into my confidence.

No doubt the natural light of my rooms, no exaggerated skies or hidden caves, heartened each wounded soul from flying away or hibernating to an unreachable place. They each listened to my nudging ("What do you think is the problem?" / "How do you think you might fix it?") and talked. Sometimes the eyes of new clients wandered to the books I'd written (*Non-rules to Atomic Love / Make Your Happy / It's You, Never Me / Who's the Idiot Now?*) and it was easier to retrieve their trust.

"Three marriages that didn't take. Spoils of war."

Do you mean scars?

"I ate a whole chocolate drip cake. Tall, fluffed up, slathered with cocoa cream. Bite after bite, a whole twenty-eight centimeters of it. Then I pushed a finger in my throat."

How does that make you feel?

"The pot was boiling but all I heard were the water's screams."

How often do you hear the screaming water?

"He looks right through me. They call me dude, mate. My own children."

Does this make you feel unhappy, enraged, or pathetic?

"I change them like socks, sometimes three in a night. I swipe right. All the time. Strangers, but one spliff and the sex is five-dimensional."

Become conscious of your thoughts. Everything you think, say, or feel becomes your reality. Pause, impartial gaze. *Tell me more.*

The latter was Ross, fresh out of his teens. A clean-shaven, hazel-eyed wreck falling in and out of casual addictions: sex, drugs, and alcohol. There was Jazz, a baby-faced Jezebel with swollen peach lips: the voluptuousness of her body resisting to acknowledge her mental deficiencies. There was Mo, he'd give anything to be young again. Hair everywhere (his ears, his arms, brows like thickets): his were thorough commitment issues arising from childhood abandonment. Oboe-sounding Reed was rasp in her insistence to find a problem with everyone but herself: her voice could raise to piercing, and she became just as challenging to contain as the musical instrument. She was the screams in the water.

And that was the problem: my clients were red hotted with emotion that spilled out in obesity, money problems, conflict avoidance, and so forth. It was overwhelming if not exasperating. I almost wished for a psychopath: glib and gold-eyed, callously parasitic yet cold. Emotionally empty. Psychopaths were Homophones—elegant, unemoting. Liturgical or secular classics. Never jazz or funk.

None of my clients were this. I thought of them in four classes: Mixoldians—downright melancholic. Dorians—hopefully sad. Microtonals—even temperament on the surface, but it took just a hair trigger to torrent the dam of excitement or despondence. Pentatonics —layered and complex.

Adelaide was a Mixoldian. So when she left, I was ready, truly ready, for the pop-up on the screen. It promised an eXplo. A gallivant to unravel my deepest wants. Did I know what I wanted?

"Click me. Now!" A heartbeat on the screen.

I am a sponge.

In my line of work—if indeed it *was* my line of work—it was too easy to be wanted. Clients were vulnerable. They gave themselves to understand themselves but ended up thinking they understood *me*. Passive listening isn't suited to everyone, but even in the most advanced practitioner it also absorbs. I made myself a promise to never mix business with pleasure because no pleasure came out of my business. But I was always of the disposition that rules were made to be broken, and the neon light that flickered across Floral's face advertised that aplenty.

I had taken her to the eXplo because I was chicken. Floral was so Pentatonic she might as well have had scales. A hard shell that had taken me a while to separate but which held an interesting core. Floral was cured before she even came to my clinic, but sought ratification of that resolve. She was so complex she couldn't trust herself not to undermine her own decisions. Floral could simultaneously see—and *agree*—both sides of any argument. It made decision-making almost impossible, but she always welcomed the opinion of an outsider. When I told her she was cured she accepted that finality. I knew it wouldn't be an outcome she would query. Her problems—and whatever they *had been* I couldn't even remember—were gone. If she did argue with herself over that acceptance, she certainly never told me.

My clients were rarely cured. Who made cures for birth warts? They came, they spoke, they were conquered. Until the next time. But Floral ... I knew I could obviate any risks in being associated with her. And so began that little relationship.

What I didn't expect from her was:

"I lost my koala!"

"You what?"

Neon-flickered tears strobed down her face like cats dancing in puddles. The two-headed variety, those with tuxes, top hats, canes, and tails.

I pulled her head onto my shoulder so she couldn't see my confusion, mentally scrolling through all her avatars until I came to a conclusion.

"The one riding your backpack, right?"

She looked up, gratified. "I'm so happy you remembered."

I was happy enough to have guessed. I thought back to the little mite, which I'd always assumed was some kind of 3D decal. "You thought a lot of him, I know," I said, making it up as I went along. I began to wonder if I'd become immune to the signs of taking my work home with me. This wasn't what I had planned for the evening.

"I was scammed!"

I waited to hear the explanation but the exclamation echoed in the depths of a pause. I put myself on hold. Had I created in Floral a flaw because I wanted to be adored? No, I remembered this was real. I pinched myself and then I pinched her to make sure.

"Ow!"

"Sorry, Floral. You were getting hysterical there."

She calmed herself down by sweeping a gaze over the eXplo. Everything we both desired was spread out before us apart from the understanding that together we both had all we needed.

Sometimes surrender is the only option. The Uber windows refuse to close. The passenger doors stay mismatched, one leather, the other felt. Minimal music: the driver's breathing. A giant pause in a trip across the city whose batteries are dead. You worry the phone, but spies line each windowsill. Litter strewn over the streets. Each key press is a footprint, an option of paranoia. The driver's breathing is scattered trumpets. Is there a connection? Well, you never know if the address exists. The phone rings. You let it ring. Later you'll file it under missing persons struck by thought in a beautiful moment of loaded hope inside a nightclub in this solar system. Borrowed faces. Is there an apocalypse?

Anybody with half a brain understood the perils of taking work home. Mixing business with pleasure. I was used to lonesomeness. Doing things solo. Even my office had no receptionist—I retrieved my clients myself, smiled reassurance as they fidgeted or pretended to be fine. But my clients were emotionally fucked and, frankly, so was I. Perhaps it was a curiosity that first nudged me to indulge Floral in the eXplo during our psyche session.

Click me. The ticker happened in my office PC for the first time when Floral came up with that lost-my-koala wail. There it was on the screen, the black-market game, having networked itself from my bedroom to my office. Even as I wondered what fantasies it would unravel if Floral clicked it and if I was open to witness the fantasies, I indulged the game for us both.

I took Floral's hand, led her to my desk. "I want you to see this."

Click me. Now.

She studied the screen for a moment and clicked.

The pop-up dissolved in a rainbowed confetti. Suddenly on the screen was a doe-eyed koala. It was a relief to see the koala, not a leather-clad dominatrix straddling a whip. Floral clicked on it again, and we watched, mesmerized, as the koala unzipped its skin, and stood all pink and shiny on the screen. Floral clicked once more, and skin fell off the skeleton.

"Tell me your deepest belief," my words almost a whisper, my face a breath from Floral's neck.

She trembled even as she stammered out her words, eyes on the naked skeleton still. "I'm down to earth … reliable. But people are dogs. They are always biting … even when I'm kind and quiet. Even when I am sensitive to their needs … all they do is snarl and display yellow, vicious teeth."

"What kind of dog is your husband Earl?"

Rules were made to be broken, and even the most resistant client—Ross did not resist—once unraveled by the eXplo, was susceptible to the pinch that spread our need to a place beyond hysteria.

For Floral, the koala associated or dissociated with a dog. For Ross—unsurprisingly—it was a rabbit, mating multiple times a day, undone by the shadow of an eagle soaring the skies with wings spread out. I imagined that for Adelaide the confetti might unveil a horse. Not a racehorse, perhaps just a draft horse. And that it was a boar, squealing and grunting, that would break her to open herself up to my pinch. But, by then, after years of eXplo, I'd long detached it from my office. I'd made sure every time that the internet was off during my sessions. The associative guilt of what happened when my clients unveiled their insecurities, nudged by the eXplo, was by now too big. Even I wasn't immune to a conscience. The mathematics wasn't right. Call it malpractice: I could lose my license. Here's what I reckoned: No internet = no virtual interface. The eXplo couldn't square root into my office, multiply itself by itself into my sessions. Or so I thought.

Imagine my astonishment when *Click me* blinked right there on the screen, straight after Adelaide. And I was alone, no client. It was as if it was all in inverse. That I, not Adelaide, needed to differentiate some layers. Would you have clicked?

Well, I did.

Confetti on the screen dissolved to display—not a koala, rabbit or draft horse, or whichever emotive trigger existed for my client—an address. And the Uber driver did find it, the destination was a night-club polluted with sound throbbing into the street like an apocalypse was coming.

I wondered why the eXplo had brought me here. How did it think it would unpeel my layers with metal, rap, and rock, all volume turned up?

New and old stars, a spiral of galaxies. Formations in a dance of rings around an oval. You follow paths but to what ellipses? Random motions, spinning, spinning. Is it remembrance or mimicry of what lives within?

The driver pulled off, abandoning me to a hammer of music that was spiked with wailing. I looked at my bearing: 200 meters from Flinders Street towards Spring Street. Behind me, a wire fence—if you climbed it, you'd plummet to the rail tracks where slow trains pulled into the station's tunnel and to the platforms. Ahead, between me and a closed Indian restaurant, was an abandoned tram stop. I couldn't see the nightclub but could certainly see its sound. Blobs of strobe light and patterns of zigs and zags, then random blots and bursts to a beat on the other side. It was beginning to pour. By the time I made up my mind, crossed the road, and walked around the Indian restaurant, the skies were gushing down.

The bouncers, sour sorts with serious muscle guns on their arms, looked right through me. I slipped past them into a doorway. Nine windy steps down from the hammer of beats on the street, I found myself in a basement of inside music that wasn't so loud. It was like the notes and mismelodies had escaped from themselves and the basement, and spilled into the streets. What remained was a husk, the memory of a song. A haze of peals, a prowl of wails. A sound of something you didn't know but wished was deep. A whistle of broken lips, a tap of bones. Keening, wailing. On occasion, a drum. Clapping, too, vibrating to a shuffle groove.

Forms and images bobbed on the dancefloor. Ellipses, parabolas, three-dimensional polyhedrons. Flat faces, egg faces, cones, and cylinders. People with shut eyes, moving bodies. Faces fading, assembling. They turned from me when I approached them. Reassembling. I floated to lost music in a sense of beauty and terror. Weightlessness. A whiff of smoke, metal, blood. The basement was packed yet unpacked. I was surrounded yet alone. Dry from the rain but alone. I was here and now. I was absent.

Suddenly he grabbed my elbow. He was there, dancing with me. He was here, he was there—his fresh young face, eyes lit with mischief. We were tight. We were tense. We were fluid. Assembling, reassembling. She was back, she was forth—dark sweet notes of her perfume, blue-black hair in a fringe across her face. They were handsome. They were dangerous. I was playing a game, and it was deadly.

The music reverberated. Tremors in my soles. We cut shapes. Strobed. I went in to their out and vice versa. The fluidity of existence. A dance to the beginning of time.

Equally, flailing. Tumbling down a green grassy bank, collecting moss. Or a mote of dust in a Catherine wheel caught in a lazy centrifugal force. Sometimes a lone argyle sock in a washing machine, spin cycle set to repeat. Or a piece of colored kaleidoscope glass, fitting, refitting. The skein of a bubble in a washing-up bowl: soapsud galaxies.

I couldn't pin an identity on my dancing partner. Friend, foe, or a shift of something in between. The music rushed towards us before receding, creating space that only we could inhabit: the undertow of a wave. As though cocooned in a cave I watched surrounding air solidify, enclosing us further, twin kernels inside a nut. Abruptly, the music stopped.

The other, my dancer, was static in their movement but fluid in their form, as though a projector played alternating male/female imagery across the smooth white marble of a statue. I sought identification but found none. Glanced at my own hands, my body, expecting to see similar shimmerings of light, coalescing in confirmation, yet I was intact, pinned to myself as if I were the proven suspect in an identity parade. I couldn't change the person I had become.

Urgent hands tugging my elbow. It was a child in a tux and bow tie. Curls on his head. Big, brown eyes.

"Come," he piped with urgency.

We ran in slow motion, a child pulling my hand. We filtered in and out of shapes that turned into Hellenic statues: octopus-limbed, hydra-headed monstrosities. I drifted past in fear and fascination, chasing along corridor after corridor of a funfair, or a museum, or an album of ancestry. I was younger, smaller, uncertain where my body started or ended. I was liquid, memory fading, nothing filling gaps. Now we stood outside a crimson door lettered in gold with a name: *Messier 94*. In the abstraction and dissonance, I looked at the child gazing up at me with big puppy eyes full of windows and mirrors that showed I was an adult once more. I put a hand to my half-familiar face. Sensed the presence of a ghost that wasn't leaving, with me casting its shadow. I felt the contours of my dry throat and knew with no answers or detail that I wasn't asleep.

"Are you a muffin or a crumpet?" asked the child.

"A muffin, of course," I said absently.

The child laughed, a soft sound of tiny bells, and ran off barefoot.

I put a hand to the gleaming knob, but the door creaked ajar, anticipating me. I paused a moment, then entered.

The surrounding space was darkened yet gradually came into light. A rushing into consciousness. Furniture flickered then faded into existence. A bed, freshly made white sheets with the coverlet turned down. A beech wooden bedside cabinet, built into the wall. A Bible visible within a closed drawer, transparent until the images formed securely around it. A door to the side, leading to the bathroom. Dark yellow curtains shut out the night. Carpet formed around my feet, lifting one, then the other, until it was uniform on the floor. I recognized this place because I had seen it a hundred times in cities replicated across the world and all over eXplo: a typical hotel room. As sexless as to be androgynous until androgyny became the fetish.

The figure opposite remained in a struck pose. The eXplo had taught me interaction was necessary. A click or switch to start the game. What perspective for this interface? I walked to the hotel door, placed my vision to the fish-eye, caught corridor curves and little else. My ear against the wood faintly detected muffled music, as though the outside were unimpeded, was continuing beyond the present within which I was trapped. Or was "trapped" too strong a word, "contained" more accurate? I was held in motion, with reality in liquid formation around me. Walking to the curtains I parted them to reveal a starless night. Vantablack. An absence of existence.

It reminded me of the attributes of my patients, blank canvases for personalities revealed through questioning or existing images seeking coloration to make them complete. In each case, they held their individual music, a theme tune, a walk-on song. Music was the constant that transcended the visual parameters of the game. Music was *outside* the game. But it wasn't a game, of course, it was reality in the currently known galaxy.

I walked around the frozen figure. The images projected onto its body—or more accurately, emanating *from*—were in 360 degrees. Each contour, every crevice, was in some way pixelated, a future century *Illustrated Man* from the Ray Bradbury twentieth-century classic. No doubt shortly something would happen. It felt like the image was charging, storing energy, seeking the power for the transformation to physically bring them into the space I already occupied. The fact that I was here was the clue to my identity. The fact that the figure wasn't quite here was key to the puzzle.

Flashes in my head, as if outside of here we were still on the dance-floor. I could feel the peripheries of my flesh moving, as though I were a skin within skin. A sensation of airflow anchored me to reality, tiny fluctuations indicating the reverberations of music. Whatever I had to solve required resolution in here, before I was snapped out to the other world, discarded and hurt.

I reached with my right hand until it was perpendicular to my body, and touched the shoulder of the faceless body facing me.

The important parts of the human body's vibration frequency are generally located at about 3 Hz–17 Hz. According to the International Standard ISO 2631, in the vertical vibration of the human body, the sensitive range is located in 6 Hz–8 Hz.

With heightened sensitivity, I felt a pulsing energy race through me. It stemmed from the tremors of my fingers on that shoulder. My whole body shook inextricably in mechanical vibration and shock, and I felt or anticipated the creature's awakening.

What I didn't anticipate was the voice, so full of hollow and empty like a broken wind instrument. And the lamenting words from somewhere in a nebula of bulges and rotations. Head lighter than helium, I shifted in and out of myself and swooned into a swallow of explosions as the words, pregnant with echo, touched me with the anomalous sweetness of honeyed lips or divine wings:

"What is the problem from your point of view?"

My point of view.

Words flowed out of my mouth as music—metal, jazz, and blues. An outward manifestation of inner turmoil.

In therapy, I'd advised my patients to change their vibration frequency: *Become conscious of your thoughts. Everything you think, say, or feel becomes your reality*.

In gaming, perspectives defined player interactions, including first-person, third-person, top-down, isometric, flat, side-view, and text-based characterization. Improvisation, syncopation, swing. So, what *was* my reality, my point of view? Ellipses. Parabolas. Polyhedrons.

I'd always thought the *X* in Dr X represented the unknown. But in some games, an X was an action button, in others X meant to quit.

The blood on the door handle—did I want an answer to it?

Or was it always and forever mine?

I closed my eyes.

XX

STILL SHE VISITS

YOU REMEMBER when you were eleven or twelve, hands fumbling with a folded cloth. The tingle of a sore nipple, the claws of muscle cramp. Each pang in your pelvis was a sword that hacked away your childhood.

Your mother waltzed into your grave-sized room. It was tiny enough to hold two coffins and a row of ghost feet. It always felt haunted. Mamm brought in her rage and suspicion in a growl that said, "What mischief are you plotting?" even though the words were different: "Tidy your room yet?" Furrows on her forehead, her no-nonsense gait ... all now just a memory in fragments.

It was your little sister Mokgosi—her name means "a call for help" —who used her body to shield your secret from your mamm. Why it had to be a secret, you don't know; maybe it was to stop your mother from fraying your ears with threats about boys. How they took everything you gave, then broke you even though you were empty. How they sauntered whistling to a forever place, leaving you with mouths to feed, tiny mouths that couldn't tolerate hunger.

"Loosen, Mamm. Just ease." Mokgosi's calming words stood in front of your stained pad and your mother, ever grouchy like a buffalo.

Mamm looked harder at your sister and your blocked self, still with rage and suspicion, but she left the room without a word, and that didn't happen all that often. You looked at Mokgosi. She looked at you. She gave you a clean pad and soaked your blood in salted cold water, washed the nasty cloth with her bare hands, because money, money, money. There was no money to take to a shop and buy tampons.

It was then that you understood your sibling bond, even though before that you were street dogs—the way you fought. This new love moved you through bad things, like when your mother left, not just your room but this time for good.

It's an undying love that makes you see through the hollow in Mokgosi's eyes full of dusk, so you can unsee the guts like strings falling out of her mouth, her ears. Her silent aura telling you like a movie that she's dead, please be honest.

"Sorry, I ..." You clang pots, bang doors in your apartment in East Melbourne. *Thump-thwack-clang-bang*. How can you be honest to such loss?

But still, Mokgosi visits.

Segomotsi—your name means "a comfort" in Setswana. Few people here know you by that name; they call you Seggie Slacken—the Aussie you married.

It's years since you traveled home. Botswana will be a stranger, the village of Lejwana even more. But with your parents gone, and without your sister Mokgosi, what's left to call home?

A girl waits opposite you at the shrink's office. She flicks through pages of a brand-new issue of *Women's Interest*. She's chewing gum. Flick, chew. The receptionist ignores you both.

You consider the receptionist, her face sharp as a pin, her nose and ponytail equally harsh. Back home, you would chat to strangers like old friends: ask about their cows, their goats, their children. Here, folk don't do that.

The psychiatrist who retrieves you has dimples. Her pensive face is complete with lines: forehead lines, crow's feet at the sidelines, marionette lines that run straight upwards from the corners of her mouth. Her room is pristine, bland colors unable to touch your moods. Her leather couch is familiar, wears an easy look like the coin-slotted massage sofa at the Jam Factory in South Yarra.

You ignore Mokgosi, her hollow eyes, oozing entrails, sitting in the corner of the room. The settee in which you recline, face up to the bland ceiling, smells synthetic. Nothing like the dusky cowhide on Uncle Kopano's chairs in Lejwana, unbleached skin, and hair that smells of wet mud. This leather is coffee-colored, café latte.

"How are you?" Dr. Bland. Her voice matches the insipid room.

"How is she in this room?" you say.

"How is who in the room?"

"There. Can't you see?"

"What would you like me to see?"

"She looks like death but smells fresh and sweet like gazania."

Silence.

"She was like that in life, you know. Bright yellow, hot orange, cheery purple, her temperament, sometimes the clothes she got from mtumba—second hand. Face of the sun, unfussy, everything she wore just fit right."

Silence.

"Dainty, but she was the stronger of us two. With a mother like ours who had to fight for everything she got, so much that she mistook her children for combat, you needed a Mokgosi standing with a water bottle and a towel in your corner. So here she is, fully here, to fight my demons—only now she's one too. All wretched to look at, but there's strength in her scent. Sweet mango. Sometimes durian."

You leap into the swimming pool at the aquatic center. Mokgosi dangles her feet in the water, makes you touch them each turn at the wall before you somersault. It feels like a call for help, but whose—yours or Mokgosi's?

A week.

"Is Mokgosi in the room with us today?" asks Dr. Bland.

"Right there. Same corner."

Mokgosi who always stood by your side, but you're the one who got away. It was curiosity for the world and a scholarship that put you on a plane, and away, away you flew.

"What's she looking at?" asks Dr. Bland.

"You."

"What's she thinking, do you know?"

"I guess—why you? She was always there for me."

"And how do you feel right now?" asks Dr. Bland.

"Cross," you say.

"Cross—because your sister is looking at me?"

"Because work sucks. Been thinking to leave."

Silence.

"Employee assistance program, bereavement leave on tap, cards, flowers ..." you say.

"I'm glad you took EAP—that's why you're here," says Dr. Bland.

"How can a plant so rugged be so beautiful? It grows in extreme heat, tolerates any drought, climbs out of the hardest earth to splay in vibrant colors ..." You choke.

Dr. Bland hands you a tissue.

A week.

"Surprised?" Dr. Bland. Sometimes she's like this, prods you with a question. "Why so? You say Mokgosi surprised you?"

"When Mamm left ... her leaving was not the kind of walk away our father did: *Grabbing cigarettes, be right back.* A beast in the wind swallowed him whole, no one saw him again. No, Mamm's leaving was the kind that happens where shadows reach into sleep and take away a loved one." All that fighting the world, finally it took its toll. "She ate dinner one night, rested her head on a pillow, closed her eyes, and never woke up."

"So how has your sister surprised you?"

"Mokgosi doesn't hurt like when Mamm died."

Mokgosi slips from her corner, her gazania bloom smell tightly closed—today she's odorless. She shuffles to the settee in which you recline. Traces with her gnarled finger a tear that brooks its way around your nose to the edge of your lips.

"If Mokgosi doesn't hurt," says Dr. Bland, "then why are you crying?"

A week.

"Do you know that the gazania flower doesn't bloom on a dark or stormy night?"

"Is that how you feel today?" Dr. Bland. "Dark and stormy?"

"I feel far."

"What do you mean?"

"Too far to mourn."

"Why didn't you go to Botswana when she was sick?"

"Work, stuff."

"How are you dealing with being far now?"

"I sent money. WorldRemit. To help with the funeral."

Silence.

"But they didn't need it. Took them a week, a whole week for Uncle Kopano to collect it. The chief is a friend of my family. He paid for everything: hospital bill, ivory-finish coffin. They didn't need my money."

"How does that make you feel?"

Mokgosi's hollow eyes full of dusk pouring into your soul. "What do you expect?"

Silence.

"No Tobin Brothers Funeral services in Lejwana, you know. Nobody to wash her. Nobody saying to you, *How would you like to make your coffin look?* Or, *We'll send out the funeral notice to your friends.* It's the women who washed her, dressed her. Put lipstick on her face. Put eye shadow, angel face. Put her in a white dress with a shiny coat. No curls in her hair; they put on a headdress."

Silence.

"There were drums, huge drums, Uncle said. Doomba-doo! Doomba-doo! Dodoomba-doo! Doo! Doo! Doodoodoo! The whole village was together, they farewelled her like a queen."

Mokgosi, in her corner, smiles at the memory.

"All of Lejwana at her doorstep. They sang, they danced, they drank. They feasted: platters of meat and rice. Chief Dikeledi paid for it. People ate fit to burst."

Silence.

"I feel rubbish."

Mokgosi is on the settee—how did she get there so quickly? She's cradled to your breast. Her aura is red with splashes of hot pink. Her scent, dear gods, her scent. An overwhelming sweetness that reminds you of a wedding.

"What do you regret the most?" says Dr. Bland.

"Being 7000 miles from Mokgosi's grave. Far, far from home ..."

Mokgosi strokes your cheeks through the sadness.

"I didn't even keep the Aussie." Your smile is cynical. "Slacken. The divorce was a slap in the face for him, fourth year of our marriage. No wonder he went mean after that, the slap still ringing."

A week.

Today Mokgosi looks like your mother: the rage, the suspicion, black fog swirling from her empty eyes. Furrows on her head, a no-nonsense gait.

"How are you today?" Dr. Bland. She sits in a comfortable silence, palms flat, parallel to her thighs. Sometimes she sprawls her arms casually on each armrest.

"Angry. ANGRY."

"Talk to it," says Dr. Bland. "Talk to your anger."

Acha! Stop! Mokgosi is shaking her head, making a gargling noise. She's rocking in a corner, back against the wall like Mamm did in the kitchenette when your father evaporated.

"Why don't they call it what it is? What it is IT IS!"

"Why don't they call what?" asks Dr. Bland.

"What it is IT IS she died of."

"What do you want to call it?"

Mokgosi leaps. Her scream is full of echoes, her arms outstretched to muffle or strangle you. Entrails like tongues rush from the yawn of her gobbling mouth.

"Break the circle of silence. It's not malaria. It's not pneumonia. It's not tuberculosis." Hands on your throat, you can't breathe,

breathe. But the words fall out of your mouth: "It's AIDS. AIDS. AIDS!"

Mokgosi's fading cry, *Arrggggh* ... Then she puffs out, leaving behind a sickly sweet smell of formaldehyde.

Your wet face against Dr. Bland's breast.

A week.

"No more Mokgosi in the room?" asks Dr. Bland.

You shake your head. "No more."

You're surprised that something is changed in Dr. Bland, in how she speaks now. She talks differently. A slant in her vowels, a trail as if they're cursive with consonants. There's color in Dr. Bland. Texture.

"What do you want to talk about today?" asks Dr. Bland.

"Like what?"

"Tell me anything." Each vowel has its sound, like a sixth sense.

"I made hard decisions, the ones that made me stay. It wasn't the lightness of bills—he was more expensive to keep than me alone. I married an Aussie, but it wasn't for the fondness in his touch. Kissing him was like smooching carrion, the sex as impersonal as a bus driver's glance at dismounting passengers. I don't know why I stayed. All night as he snored, I heard sirens. *Do you have a moment?* they sang. *Tell us your name.*"

"And what's your name?" Cursive words, the tongue lingers.

You're not sure whether it's you or Dr. Bland who has changed.

"My name is Segomotsi—it means 'a comfort' in Setswana."

You lie in bed, unable to sleep. You remember the hurt you forgot. The day Mokgosi died, your sense of loss was so keen, it pierced holes into your gut, and cannonballs entered those holes. You flick on the lights, look at the white of the ceiling speckled with the cream of the apartment sprinkler, a fire safety gadget with circular ridges and protrusions. Three silver hooks fasten the translucent plate covering the bulb.

Had to happen in March?

Death is easier in November—New Year around the corner. Come January, you set your mind to new thinking. You leave death with the year gone. Sucks in March; you have to live with death the whole year.

You look at your phone: 6 a.m.

It's Saturday.

Aquatic center, you prefer the outdoor pool. You swim like the physio instructed: "When you turn to breathe, level your cheek with the water surface, not nose up." You agree with the physio: this way is less strain on your neck.

Every day is winning and losing. Sometimes more win than loss, a little more now. She still visits, Mokgosi. Unfolding in bright colors of the gazania. She's an African daisy and, like all daisies, she's complete in herself. Gazanias, like tall grasses, just more radiant, appear anywhere. There she is luminescent in the water, shimmering with the waves as you swim. Hers is a big kiss, florets and golds spreading with each stroke. Now I'm a bigger bloom, she says. Her voice buzzes rich with low notes. You should see, she says in her resonant bassoon. It's a starburst here.

You swim, swim. Sweet mango and durian: her scent in the waves.

Water enters your nose, your mouth, just enough not to unsettle. Breathing cheek level with the water, you like it. It is almost like a water hug. The sun is playful. She patterns the base of the pool with her rays. A white ray bounces off a window to reflect on your tinted goggles as you breathe. Your face is in the water. The sun's rays are a comfort, like your name. The sun feels intimate.

Like Mokgosi's gaze.

A week.

Silence.

Silence.

"Tell me anything." Dr. Bland.

"Anything."

She smiles.
Silence.
Silence.
"I know to see when I'm drowning," you say.
"Good. Make sure you keep swimming."
You smile.
Silence.
Silence.

A VISIT IN WHITECHAPEL

IT WAS A BLEAK and blustery morning. It was the day the earth shook, and aliens fell from the sky. At first, we thought it was a meteor. Then we thought it was a shooting star. Something glowing rocketed down the horizon and landed in sudden light and a thunderclap. There it was, smack in the middle of Buck's Row—a smoking crater.

By the time the people of Whitechapel had spilled out from Yeoman's Yard, where the Glitter stood, from Raven's Row where Mr Reaper owned an antique shop, from Settles Street near the cop shop, and all the way from Mill Yard where a misty old church full of rot now stood, the gorge from the fallen fireball was shaking and groaning as if birthing a terrible beast.

The gorge went silent and stirred up a stampede, people moving away, not towards, as something stranger began to unfold. A young man of unusual darkness—he wore tight pants and a cloak with a cape, just like the wizards in folklore—climbed out of the smoke. His eyes were weapons—they put a hole in your soul.

He turned, and the crowd gasped. Reaching out of the gorge was a woman's hand. He took it, helped her out, and we saw her face. She, too, was a person of color, her skin more chestnut than his ebony. She was wholly exotic. Her head was wrapped in blue and gold, an elaborate headdress that coned and finished in a fringe. While he was slender, she was comfortably rotund and moved gracefully, flowing in kaleidoscopic robes—unlike our everyday tunics of metallic hue.

She cast the dazzle of her long-lashed gaze at the crowd, at us. We stood entranced. Hers were the eyes of a unicorn. She blinked and at once the ashy gorge disappeared. In its place stood what appeared to be a crystal tower filled with animals, beasts of a kind we'd never seen before. The animals we knew all flew, and they were seasonal. They came with the blood moon, the twin moon, the blue moon, an eclipse, a comet or a Venus transition. They were unicorns, honed and shimmering with enchanted dust. They were lightning birds with long, black beaks and long, long legs. They were cockatrice, serpent-like with a bird's head, and they heralded a message, often of a good birthing like the night we came into the world. Griffins, with their talons and wings—if they came, a death would happen. Last time one appeared it chose to land on a spire. The skyscraper upon which the spire stood tumbled and fell flat on my father. The sphinx—you were lucky if you saw one in broad daylight, but it brought good fortune, unlike the Pegasus, a winged creature, fully cursed. The last time one was seen was centuries ago, and it used the black plague to eradicate a whole monarchy. Only the royals perished. The Metropolitan Police brought order, and our father had been one of them.

But these animals gazing down at us from the crystal tower of the aliens, they were not unicorns or griffins, lightning birds or cockatrice. The sight of them was like a mirage, faces in dancing water. We were curious to investigate the marvel. But by this time the Metropolitan Police had arrived in their black sapphire tarragons that roared a big sound from deep in their bellies, so loud we couldn't ignore it. We saw Uncle George—he used to work with our father—a good sort. The alien turned her unicorn eyes on him, and Uncle George was smiling —we didn't think he'd be arresting tonight—so we dispersed with the crowd.

We raced up a float of stairs to our apartment. We went to tell Mum about the aliens. But she was levitated, folded into herself, an invisible spike in her heart, and it was turning, turning, hollowing out a tomb inside her body.

She was getting over a second break-up with O.

Before the earth shook, before the aliens, we waved to Dora in her fairy-winged dress full of sapphire ribbons. She waved back, a tangle of emerald lilies from a Kensington boutique bobbing in her combed-out hair. A thousand brushes, O always said as he tenderly drew out each strand with the mystical brush from her princess dresser.

Mum smiled briefly at O, looked away swiftly, and a frown replaced the smile as our ride arrived. There was no hint of softness on her face from just before, at the door, when she brushed O's lips with hers, when she clung to him for no greater than a moment. He stood tall at the doorway, head almost touching the dome, and watched as we pulled into the horizon with a tarragon-ride woman who was the no-nonsense kind, for all the burgundy and gold tint splashed on her metallic conveyance.

Mum stayed silent across the sky, even as we nagged: "Are we there yet? Are we, are we?" Normally she'd say, "Not yet, mate," or "What's going on?" This time she didn't notice. Her stare was ardent along the vista as if fretful the clouds might melt in the London sky. *Zeus,* she cursed an ermine-white tarragon, or the man in it when the tarragon swerved into our path but flew way too leisurely ahead of our ride.

Mum's voice was wet when she asked if we'd like some shakes, and we said yes.

"Do you mind a detour?" she said to the tarragon-ride woman.

"Cost you double," said the no-nonsense sort.

We got shakes from the fly-thru: a peanut butter cup and a rocky road delight, one with molten cherry sauce, the other with whipped chocolate butter. Mum was clearly grumpy because she snapped, "Keep it down, will you?" in the ride. We stopped pulling at each other and took from her our molten delights as the attendant with a green leprechaun tunic and a matching hat handed them over. Before we even asked, Mum said we could eat in the tarragon, never mind the no-nonsense woman who cast us a wicked eye. Soon as we got out, Mum spat on her hands and wiped grime off our faces—oh, didn't we thrash!

Before we stepped into the apartment up a float of stairs, so unlike O's grounded house, Mum turned squarely to us. She wore a brave face like she was about to take a pill, a jab or something, and said, "What happened with O, it wasn't your fault."

As people went about their days, nursing or teaching or engineering or developing, Mum still cradling her wretched heart, we stole to what was once Buck's Row, then a smoking crater, now a crystal tower full of exotic beasts.

There stood the tower, right where we left it. No one was going in; the animals were not coming out. But the place was wide open, no doors to lock people out. We stood at the threshold for a minute, the crystals on its outer walls shimmering and beckoning us in, and there was no sight of Uncle George or the rest of the Met.

"Look what I found." The alien woman's voice was a song, the sound of a bird, the music of the moon, playful in her pretty throat. Her lashy unicorn eyes swallowed us in their gaze. She stood at the mouth of the tower, arms akimbo. She took in our tunics. "Are you soldiers, then? Little Romans, perhaps?"

"Who are Romans?" we piped.

"Great engineers, soldiers and constructors," she said in her melodic voice. "They lived in beautiful houses surrounded by slaves. They also killed people in a most terrible way."

"What are slaves?"

"People without choice. But you two appear to have it in plenty, no?" She took our hands, "Come," and guided us into the tower.

Inside it was like nothing we imagined. The animals were not standing at crystal windows and gazing at Whitechapel. They were out in the wild. Indeed, the tower was not a tower. It was a meadow swathed in lush green grass. It was vast land speckled with deeply blue lakes and some murky ones. This world bore a remoulade of creatures and a scent of something exquisite. It reminded us of Mum when she was light on her feet, buoyant, no mourning in her exquisite face, in her soft lips that kissed our brows to sweet sleep.

"My name is Babirye," the alien woman said in that dawn chorus voice. "And this," the man appeared as if from a shadow, "is my brother Kato."

"We're twins, we're twins," we piped with excitement. "Are you twins?"

Babirye laughed. Her big necklace of shells danced on her neck.

"Actually, yes." She caught our interest on her throat. "Cowrie shells," she said.

We blinked for a spine-tingling moment, filled with a sense of anticipation. "Are you gods?"

"Grief, no," she said in words like music.

"Why do you bring them here?" It was Kato. He was arresting, full-voiced.

"These ones bring no harm," she sweetly sang, and skipped with the lightness of a sprite despite her flowing robes and headgear. "These are Wanyama," she told us, and waved towards the beasts that were scattered in the exotic wilderness.

We met Fisi, a spotted thing with small black eyes, standing ears and short back legs. He looked like a thief and laughed as we passed.

"Don't mind him," said Babirye.

We met Tembo and her big long nose, big floppy ears, wide, wide legs. She had eyes so gentle. We met Duma, a sleek beautiful thing with a pretty long tail that swished as she paced around us. She purred, closed her eyes, when Babirye stroked her chin. We met Kinyonga who changed colors like a diorama. He didn't mind us, just turned flesh-colored, orange-tinted red, amaranth, lime … as he walked. Sokwe was almost human, just furry and cradling a baby that sucked from her breast. She whooped and gibbered as we neared, nearly bit us.

"A mother is always protective, no?" said Babirye. "Enough for today."

Mum was still levitated in sleep, but we woke her when Mr Reaper of the antique shop visited, and she agreed to get up and make tea. Unlike us, he never took the floating stairs. He was tall, ashy-haired, often with a walking cane, but we knew there were times, such as when he entered and left the Glitter, he didn't need the cane. His visits to Mum were occasional, and she appeared to listen to his counsel.

"The blackness will lift," we eavesdropped from the stairs. "He's a monster you don't need. Not with his moods and how he is to the children."

But nothing he said could shake her from her mood. "Now, now," we heard, and knew that Mum was crying again.

"Let me take the children for a ride."

"But what about the shop?"

"It runs itself."

We didn't like Mr Reaper's ride—his was a beaten gray tarragon peeling with paint. It shuddered, not soared, coughed, not roared. But we loved his knowledge of history, as he pointed out places.

"Right there, in the north end of what was once the Palace of Westminster, was Big Ben. It was London's iconic timepiece and it stood on a tall spiked building. People came from all over the world to see it. There," he pointed, "that used to be Winchester Palace right there, near Borough Market." The tarragon shuddered. "Right here, riverside, there used to be a giant London Eye. It was the tallest observation wheel in the whole of Europe." He looked at us keenly. "Ah! Do you remember the Tower of London?"

"Many a duke, baron, king or queen lost their heads by the axe, or by hanging from the gallows," we said.

"Yes, sometimes there was a burning. Or the infamous hanging, drawing and quartering. Others fell to their death while trying to escape the tower. Do you remember why?"

"Sometimes it took several blows to sever the head."

"Indeed. It took eleven strokes in one case. The condemned was nervous and moved. The executioner accidentally struck her shoulder. She bounded from the block, blood gushing everywhere, and the executioner chased her with his axe."

"If the axe was neat, did you die immediately?" we asked.

"Never. Do you know one can remain conscious nearly a minute until you die from lack of oxygen to the brain? Look. Once there was a traitor's gate right there, lined with impaled heads."

After the tour, we hoped he would take us to his antique shop and its jadeite dishware, and lots of shiny things, some with strings, and hear him say, "This is an antique guitar—you strum a string and it plays. This is an oboe—it's a woodwind instrument and you blow like this to make a sound ..." And slip our fingers into perfume jars and their floral fragrances of violets, lilies and lavender, their dreamy fragrances of vanilla and cinnamon, and their fresh fragrances of lemons and bergamot. And feel the books: hardcovers and paperbacks. And hear him say, "This was how people read. They opened a book and looked at its text. It was nothing like audio and story globules you touch with a finger and they tell you or show you stories."

But as we flew back over Whitechapel and crossed over the Glitter, we saw the ravenous look in Mr Reaper's eyes and knew the antique shop was not to be. Not on this day, no.

That autumn at O's wasn't fun. He was self-medicating for his migraines, doubling doses, and his mood was getting more and more grotty. His voice still held a silk note for Dora but for us it was always the growl, a bigger growl. He barked when we changed the setting in Dora's system and it went from virtual reality to alternate reality—although it worked better, he agreed later, and Dora could still play all her favorite games. After he bellowed at us in the tarragon, then turned the ride round so we went back to his house instead of soaring from Camden to Kensington as he had promised, Mum also saw he wasn't fun. She jumped out the ride soon as it landed, marched fuming into the house, and—before we could do the same—O said, *Children, stay in the ride.*

Who needed to get out to hear them tearing at each other? Horrible words, but what was said could have been worse:

"When I say anything to them, you think I'm a bully!"

"Did I say anything when you jumped at them in the tarragon? Sure, I was surprised when you turned round —"

"I'd had enough!"

"And I could see why their bobbing might annoy you —"

"And you did nothing!"

"Because you did something."

"I had to!"

"What's done is done. Already you've roared at them, and turned back the tarragon —"

"I wanted you to do something!"

"But you'd already done something!"

"And now you storm out of the ride—clearly, you're upset I did something."

"The only reason I stormed was because I was still mad at you for spoonfeeding Dora. By Zeus, O. She's not that little."

"Mad? Why would you even say that? She's never eaten so well!"

"Feed your little princess with a golden spoon!"

"Did you see how she ate all the peas?"

"My ones—they're not your biological kids —"

"You can't control them —"

"They can never do anything right, can they?"

"She ate all the peas!"

They stared at each other in astonishment, shattered by their rage.

It was then that Mum said, "We're struggling, don't you see?" Then she ordered a ride, pressed her lips on O, smiled and waved briefly before she frowned, and we were gone.

That night she sat up, startled, from broken sleep. We stroked her hair with our fingers, not a brush, and told her we took everything from our room at O's. "Even the alternate reality game *Gods of War,*" we said.

"I'm glad you took everything," she said.

"O's house was awkward," we said. "Did you see how it was awkward, Mum?"

She didn't tell us it wasn't O's house that was awkward but that it was us who had turned awkward in it because everything was by then compromised, complicated. She didn't say that all was lost, how could there be a future? She didn't tell us how the swallowing pain of loss was inside out, how—if only O knew—she was a simple call away ... But Mum understood what we didn't at the time, that sometimes love is not enough.

The next day, Babirye met our arrival at the threshold. Her headdress was speckled with flowers, yellows and reds. Her flowing robes were the color of spring, a merging of young and ancient flora. She introduced us to Digidigi, a tiny creature with a lean face. Big black eyes, slender neck. He was nimble on his feet. We met Swala, horned, wearing the eyes of a woman. Pundamilia and his pattern of stripes barked at us but continued to eat the grass, until Fisi and his clan showed, laughing like thieves. Pundamilia took flight, and Babirye did not intervene.

"It's the nature of the order, no?" she said, her words full of music. "Are you hungry?"

"Yes," we said.

She led us to a small round house made of mud, long yellow grass for its roof.

"This is a hut," she sweetly said. Its floor was pure earth. Something was cooking on a fire inside three stones. "This is a hearthstone," she cooed. "Kato must be near."

He appeared like a wish, with his cloak and weapon eyes. "Is it not enough that you take them to see Wanyama? Now they must see our beds?"

"Don't be like this, Kato," she said.

She led him outside, and we heard their arguing. His boom voice, her bittersweet notes.

"It confuses the order!" we heard him roar. "Especially tonight!"

She was subdued when she returned. As for Kato, he was gone.

"What's a bed?" we asked.

"Why?" She laughed. "Don't you sleep?"

"We levitate," we said.

"How?"

"We think ourselves to sleep and the body arranges itself in the air."

"I can't pretend to understand it, but for now, sit."

We willed ourselves to sit. Babirye looked at us, afloat on air, and laughed in astonishment. "I meant to sit on the ground, but this tells me you might also not know about chairs?"

"They're in Mr Reaper's antique shop," we piped.

"The brain is a powerful thing. Can you fly too?"

"Not so high. That's what tarragon rides are for. The metal things that fly."

"I see." She offered something white on a plate. "Try this, no?" It had the texture of potato, only sweeter like a nut. "It's called cassava."

Kato returned to the hut. His eyes stayed hostile, even as he took a cupped container made of wood. He scooped out a drink from a round-bottomed container on the floor.

"Can we have some?" we begged.

He walked out without a word.

Babirye shook her head. "Not from that pot—it's not for children."

"Why not? Why? Why?"

"That millet brew will take you places you don't want to visit."

"But we do, we do. We want to see places."

"Try this instead."

"Is it good? Is it, is it?"

"It's excellent."

It was a sweet milk, clean to swallow.

"That's from Mbuzi," she said. "You haven't met her yet, and I don't know if you will." Her lashy eyes were full of sadness, the radiance in them waned, as if she knew something we didn't. Before we asked, she said it: "Go before my brother returns from the place that brew will take him. You'll not like what you see, no?"

So, we hotfooted it, but a blue moon was glowing and we didn't go home. We raced instead down Settles Street past the cop shop and into Mill Yard. We cut a corner through Pinchin Place, then along Myrdle Street, and pounded all the way to Yeoman's Yard, where the Glitter stood. Mum said it was a place for naughty men and bad women. We climbed the walls, reached the windows. But the curtains were drawn, and they were thick. Peals of laughter, sometimes hoarse groaning, seeped under the door where we pressed our ears.

The door snapped open, and we scuttled to the shadows. Unmistakable tallness: it was Mr Reaper, without his cane. He walked briskly, as if in a hurry. We tailed him. Suddenly, he stopped outside the soap maker's cottage at Myrdle Street. We thought he had seen us, but he was just pulling out a smoke.

We hid and waited.

It wasn't long before a breathless woman joined him. The glitter in her dress, in her makeup … we knew she was from the Glitter.

"Where's the money?" she said.

"Mary Ann, I said I'll give you *after*."

"But you said it'll be quick."

"It will be."

"Where do you want me?"

"Let's go to my shop."

She giggled and fell into him. Her perfume when she passed us was something cheap that turned our noses.

He grabbed her hand. "Come quick."

We stalked them to the antique shop. But the door banged behind them, and we heard nothing. We would have stayed if we could, followed her back to the Glitter and snuck in, but a shadow cast itself upon us. We looked back in terror and saw a large creature, its eagle head and neck covered in feathers, its brown fur and furry tail. The smell, how foul! Like the small haunt we once found in our wandering by the old church. It was black and lay on its side, all four legs broken. A dirty-gray porridge oozed from the gore in its stomach, and the stench was ancient excrement or hell's cavern. The Met hauled it off and buried it somewhere, but Whitechapel reeked foul three weeks straight. To smell something so offensive again, and this time on the living … It was all the encouragement we needed to bolt homeward, and dash up the float of stairs to our apartment and into the arms of Mum, dear Mum. She was bouncy in the kitchen, light on her feet and baking banana bread. Her heart fully healed, ready for someone to break it again. She was always reaching out for something since Father's death. But did she know what? Yet seeing her so bubbly, in that instant we forgot all about the griffin we'd just seen and hugged her.

Hugged her.

Mum put floury hands on our faces. "You two will be the death of me! I've been worried sick! Where were you? I couldn't find you or Jack—the tour, when he offered it …"

"Mum! We were in the crystal tower," we cried, breathless. "But it's not a tower. And there's Fisi and Swala and Tembo and …"

"What's going on, my breathless ones? I can't make head nor tail of what you're saying. Where did the dear old man take you?"

"It wasn't Mr Reaper. It was Babirye—she has flowing robes and cloth woven on her head, and Kato—his cloak, Mum!"

"The two of you are off your heads."

We squealed at her words, clung to her tighter. Who wanted to imagine our heads on pikes along the traitor's gate?

"Hush now," she said. "If you don't tell me calmly, I promise I'll refuse to listen." She smelled so good.

So good. It was the fresh bergamot scent from Mr Reaper's antique shop.

So, we sat on her lap and told her about the meteor that was not a meteor, how it shot like a star and put a smoldering crater in Whitechapel, until the alien Babirye blinked and there was a crystal tower full of animals. But it was not a tower, and they were not cockatrice or sphinx. The place was a meadow that hosted Nyani and his blue-bottomed cousin, Kima. There was Ngumbi, the flying ant, and lots and lots of Siafu, thousands of them like walking sand. There was Mamba who liked to lie low, long and solid in the brackish part of the lake and, when she hissed at us, her jaws were spiked with a million teeth.

"And Kifaru, Kifaru," we cried. "He's a gray, fat thing with a horned snout. Such a nervous temperament!"

We talked ourselves to sleep, and poor Mum listened to it all. We were too big to carry, but tired, so tired. We levitated on our own and slept the bottomless sleep of gods after war.

The next day we floated down the stairs with Mum, and dashed to find the tower, but it was gone. In its place was yet another Whitechapel crowd and, with it, the Met. There was Uncle George. We pushed through the throng and saw, lying in a bundle on the ground at Buck's Row, a corpse—the husk of a woman from the Glitter.

"It's Mary Ann Nichols," said Uncle George to Mum. His pensive gaze turned to us. "Let's have a word now, shall we? I hear you boys have been fraternizing with some aliens." He spoke as if he doubted it. He crouched to eye level. "Let's go backwards from the end: where did they say they were headed?"

We shook our heads, teary eyed, and wondered about Kato and his weapon stare. We wondered about the sudden appearance of a griffin, a herald of death. But even as we looked at the glitter dress crumpled into the gray skeleton, a body wrapped in nothing but fossil skin, its mouth open in the silent scream of one who had lost a soul in a horrible way, we couldn't, just couldn't, imagine this was the work of –

We turned curious eyes at Mr Reaper, then back at Mary Ann discarded like garbage. But we were young.

THE FAILING NAME
(WITH SEB DOUBINSKY)

THE OVAL FRUIT, uneven on all sides even when it's ripe, is not just for eating. Spaces in the dust roads filled with reddish-brown wind are what she sees in her lost childhood. Jolainne wants to tell you, to tell anyone who'll listen, of hiding in the leaves of a mango tree, witnessing what could have been the onset of an assault.

The tree shook with the young boy's shudder, the earth hard on his face, crumbs claying his hair. As the tree sighed with the boy's cry, Jolainne yelled out, 'Arrêtez!' Stop! And hurled a mango at the man.

The mango hit—*smash!*—into the head at which it was aimed. The man zipped back his combat pants, all camouflage, his malintent with the boy extinguished. He was a scruffy white man with a mop of sun-bleached hair.

Jolainne threw another green mango that missed, as the man scuttled away. She had little time to wonder if he was a delinquent, one of the UN soldiers strutting around Kinshasa in that year of 2002, only this one gone rogue. She poised and leapt down at the trembling boy and his color of coffee.

Head tucked into his arms, his body curled into itself, he whimpered back her words: "Arrêtez. S'il vous plait." His whole body said please.

She touched his shoulder. "Viens. Je suis une amie."

"Laisse-moi," he cried. Leave me. Leave.

"Je suis une amie," she said again softly.

He took forever to uncurl, but finally looked up to confirm she was a friend. He blinked at her as if with new sight and, slowly, her words sank into his mind. *Come ... friend ... friend.* He was more shook than hurt.

The sky was so clear when she left with the boy. He gave her his hand, moist and clingy. The cry dragged in his mouth as they took to the banks of the river. There, she watched for years and years, decades, the leap of tilapia and a pile of forgotten things until he calmed himself. She touched him, just so, fingers on his nape, and felt the buzz or tingle. She didn't know whether it was the blood moon or something about the boy, or was it an inherent power inside her soul? She saw the pale blue light of a silent sorcery—perhaps a gift from the boy? His eyes, liquid tar, lit and mirrored each fish's dance. His snuffling nestled into a ditty of flame lilies in the roof of his mouth. A crimson bloom of amaryllis bulbs pulled his feet to a waltz. And they wrapped fingers and became children again.

Dusk fell and it started raining, nothing serious or intense, just a light tease that washed the wind, dripped a few leaves and opened the smell of the soil. "Mon Dieu," she said. Was that when he gave her a lock of his curls? She can't remember. What she remembers is kneading a gingerbread boy from the wet soil and willing it to breathe, but it didn't.

"Mon Dieu," he said, and ran off, his words cartwheeling in the wind: "Je m'appelle ..."

What was his name? Alain, Divin, Rivlin, Yavan? At the time he told her, it was an unfailing name. She listened to its echo in the night breeze—such was her joy, she wanted to thunder with laughter. She raced to the river the next day and the next, but he never showed. Alain, Divin, Rivlin, Yavan was gone.

And then Jolainne's mother gave her away.

She heard the fighting when it happened.

"To do what?" snapped her father.

"You have no room for wisdom," her mother's quiet voice across thin walls.

"But you have room for foolishness?"

"Marie-Toure will give Jolainne a life."

"But why?"

"Learning the world will expand her soul."

"In Paris?"

Inside the darkness of her room, Jolainne saw a flash of pale blue light. She thought of the boy with eyes of liquid tar. She fingered the pouch with his curls hemmed into her pillow.

When the door slammed with her father's rage, Jolainne knew her mother had got her way. Years and years later she would now and then wonder how a mother could refuse her child, abandon her to an aunt a whole continent away.

Sometimes Jolainne understood. Sometimes she didn't. At the time, in the naivety of her childhood, she reveled in her instant celebrity as news travelled across extended family, friends and neighbors that she was going to Paris.

People gawped at her like she was carrying an angel. Most kept a good distance, but others neared and touched her, in trust that her good fortune, unable to contain itself, would rub onto them. She could see their thinking: it was a journey of a lifetime, where she would see perhaps from a distance the landmarks of a nineteenth-century tower, an iconic cathédrale, an arc de triomphe that was a national monument, châteaux and galeries, crystalline fountains pissing water high up into the sky. And weren't there parfumeries on rue Scribe, rue Bachaumont or des Champs-Élysées? A thousand notes of Grasse rose, jasmine grandiflorum, mandarine and patchouli floating miles and miles out into the street? No one would trouble her in the city of light that flowed with crémant and its creamy nutty taste, rosés all pink and sparkling with noses of rhubarb and rose petal. Her unique origins from Kinshasa would attract easy sous that passers-by on the streets dropped on her lap, and she wouldn't even have to say her name.

Her mother put her on a five-hour bus trip and accompanied her from Barumbu in Lukunga District to Ndjili in Tshangu District. At the airport, her mother helped Jolainne check in her plastic tub, tied with cowhide rope, which carried all her belongings: a handful of batiks, rubber shoes, a lot of second-hand clothes and underwear.

"Have a good time," her mother said like a stranger before pushing her through the security barrier. But as a beefy guard rifled Jolainne's carry bag—with a toothbrush, some cassava and fried chicken, and a change of clothes—her mother had time to yell, "Make sure my grandchildren have a brown daddy."

Alain, Divin, Rivlin, Yavan ... She tries to remember his name as she fashions him under a full moon in her living room. She kneads him from clay with the curls of his hair. She has the right black buttons for his eyes. Is it the lonesomeness of twenty years in a country she still finds foreign or her mother's urging for a "brown daddy" that has summoned the pale blue light that's always been inside, the one that brings a buzz or a tingle, and makes sorcery happen?

With the plague outside and the nationwide lockdown, all is silent. The whole world is a tomb, streets haunted as a graveyard. She spits on the dough, squeezes drops of her menstrual blood from a tampon. But like before, nothing happens.

It was a midnight plane that flew two days from Ndjili to Charles de Gaulle, with two stopovers. At first when the plane taxied at speed a long time on the runway in Kinshasa, all the passengers went quiet. So quiet, Jolainne could hear the watching, heartbeats listening to the soundtrack of nothing. She worried for a moment the wheels would not lift. But they did. She watched the vessel nose towards the moon, and the lights of the world below fell away like shimmering ants, until dark clouds buried them.

Her tongue dissolved but featureless words found shape inside her fingertips. She drummed on the hand rest, keenly aware of the passenger to her left, an elderly man fully shaved and how pink, his voice like concrete, and the one next to him, a green-eyed girl with headphones. Later, a hostess came around with a tray of water. She was a lush red head, curls that fell untamed from her cap. She swung the hair with a hand to one shoulder, and the flame in it bounced rather than crackled.

The clock slowed and a siren in her head gathered speed, and she couldn't help but wonder what was at stake. Her feet were the first to go. She lost feel of the floor underneath, no pins or needles pushing inside her skin. And then it was her stomach that often blurted out endorsements, affirming fear, hunger or love—this time there was no lightness or weight, not even the flutter of wings. Her enthusiasm over Paris was a faraway thing, and the chicken and cassava were long gone. She clutched to her chest the soft pouch bearing what was left of Alain, Divin, Rivlin, Yavan.

Passengers settled to the long flight, murmurs slipped and trailed to the front, middle and rear, cartwheeled along aisles, rows and galleys in a new kind of anarchy. A trolley balancing cans of soft drink, piccolos of wines and cafetières to the brim claimed the space between no space, but Jolainne shook her head—who would pay for it? She faced out the window.

She fell asleep and there was Miriam Makeba. It was a brasserie awash with cocktail lights. Swollen with legendary patrons encircled by neat-clad waiters, a chime of cutlery and the soft buzz of chitchat. Look: Ladysmith Black Mambazo seated at the table over there in their ebony and cobalt costumes. And there! The Désira Queens in ochre-red blouses, sunflower skirts and head gear, bopping to the sounds of a song called "Umuntu". Makeba forked a mouthful of her medium-rare rib eye bathed in natural jus. The room quietened as she slipped a morsel of steak into her mouth, then sipped from a bordeaux glass of rich red wine that was no mistake, just a neat pay-off, the draft of a poem. Now Jolainne was standing in a park, carrying her fantasies but unable to walk, sending out yearnings to a paddling of ducks waddling out of a pond.

She woke up to a head swirling with so much hunger, she almost collapsed. White circles sprayed into her eyes, grew bigger and unpacked more circles that deformed into jackfruit, starfruit, papayas along garden steps with tracks to a metropolis. She looked at the menu tucked in the front seat. It promised confit fish in charred onions, caramel glaze beef in coconut curry, lemongrass coriander spring chicken, green pasta with braised beans and sprinkled with pancetta, taro cake. Jolainne nearly wept. The dryness in her head was filled with a bouquet of sweetness and musk, a final unresolved miasma that refused to restore her, to reconcile her with something big she didn't understand.

When the lush red head pushed a neat tray full of hot crepes in her face, Jolainne started to shake her head.

"You need to eat, it's a long flight," said the hostess.

"But I don't have money!" Jolainne blurted or growled.

"It's free."

She lies in bed but is not asleep—she senses the weight in her pillow. He's an invisible weight only she knows, but the shape of the gingerbread boy is still in her living room where he refused to connect to her, to unhook the language she breathed into him, and come to life. She climbs from the bed, still unable to sleep, steps into the night and scoops him with her fingers from where she left him on the windowsill. He's soft and wet. She lays him onto her palm, takes him to her bedroom where—after years of trusting and mistrusting men—she trusts his proximity, rests him in a corner of the night-eyed room. Finally, she can sleep.

After all that flying—two stopovers in Brussels and Munich, and nearly nine hours wait time in total—Jolainne finally landed the second day at 4 p.m. in Charles de Gaulle. Waiting at the baggage carousel, she panicked for a moment that her plastic tub was stolen. But there it was—who would steal it? She unroped it for a female customs officer to rifle through with gloves.

Jolainne fell out of the gates and into the fleshy arms of her auntie Marie-Toure, who was a child's height but all bosom, stomach and bum.

"Dear one," Marie-Toure poked at her ribs, "isn't your mother feeding you?"

Before Jolainne could answer, Marie-Toure swept her outside the airport, and Jolainne was finally in a car. It was a Peugeot with peeling paint, and it was unclear if it was a dirty lime or teal. Sitting in the battered thing, so gray and stale inside, she thought of old cigarettes and stale butts. The man driving it was full of hair and a beard—he called himself Mamadou. He was Auntie Marie-Toure's boyfriend.

"Travelling is learning," he said, glanced at Jolainne in the back seat. His intense eyes X-rayed her ribs. "I'll introduce you to many things."

"Advice is a stranger, Mamadou," said Marie-Toure. "Keep your eyes on the road."

He laughed, something belly-deep and rolling. "That's dope," he said, and turned on the radio.

It occurred to Jolainne that it was raining. The sound of car wipers was a giant heartbeat. Droplets hammered the roof, but the radio boomed full blast on a symphony. The baritone's eloquence was lost on the bad signal, and Jolainne thought of a dog's howl, a concert full of wretchedness, beauty stifled inside a deep, dark well.

"The music is killing us, Mamadou."

He touched the volume control, and Jolainne could have sworn he turned up the noise. But she had nothing left. Her whole body gave in to fatigue as the car burped and farted like a sick goat. It jumped down the road, blasted its horn with purpose. Finally the radio was off —Marie-Toure had taken matters into her own hands—and the Peugeot oozed a rumble from its hooded throat.

Mamadou drove blind to signs for slow down, wet road or mile post. Nothing could wheedle the car's tired wheels from lurching around corners as if in broken camber. But destiny shook it down a final road north-east of the city. It turned into a quiet street, and then another, ran down two blocks and powered off outside Lego apartments of a housing estate in an urban wasteland.

Mamadou carried the tub up sixteen flights of stairs to the tiny apartment at Porte de la Chapelle, where Jolainne quickly understood her place in the household.

"Dear one," said Auntie Marie-Toure, collapsing into a sofa. "This floor is a village. Take a broom in that cupboard."

"Let the girl rest," said Mamadou.

"There are no short cuts to the top of a palm tree. Tomorrow belongs to the people who are ready for it. Go home, Mamadou. Today you have served your purpose."

Mamadou lived in La Goutte d'Or, far away enough for Jolainne. When he said, "I'll introduce you to many things," he had different thoughts in mind.

"Auntie, why Mamadou?" Jolainne once asked.

"Dear one. We mesh."

But mesh or not, Jolainne's stomach dropped each time she heard his key in the lock. She knew the turn of his key into the apartment: push, fumble and he entered. Same way he took her, and Auntie never noticed.

The French housing estate was a colorless block of windowed cubes, blue, red and green balconies. Each home on any level was toy-sized but pregnant with roar: families, dogs, television. Blond and mauve bicycles dressed in funny bells lined the hallway that was also a garage. Tiny balconies grew potted plants in suburban lawns. Doors like soldiers—you respected their posture, no matter the noise coming from inside.

When Jolainne wakes, the sky is a diamond shimmering with a scatter of white light. In the depth of the room's silence is the rise and fall of his breathing. He's curled tight against a corner, cheeks down on the floor. His eyes are closed; he can't touch her. But their history does. She wonders at his unpolished beauty, the symmetry of his face. She listens to his aroma tucked inside the room: nutty, musty, hints of mud.

He's fetal in a bundle: closed fists, twined hips, knees and elbows. His arms and legs hug his chest. She creeps closer to peer at the grown being curved naked inward. Her own chest tugs at his helplessness as he sleeps through her curiosity.

It comes as a surprise, and then shock, when his eyes snap open. Black velvet eyes from a place full of darkness, hurled into a world too bright.

Jolainne went to a school of dirt-poor Parisians who, like her, thrived on mackerel, potatoes and bread. Sometimes they called her Lubumbashi—it didn't matter that she explained she was from Kinshasa. Sometimes they called her Pro Bono, Kunta or Coalface. Back from their taunts, or Mamadou's groping, she was wrapped in chores. She moved from living room to kitchenette and into the communal launderette. Back out again clutching a crumpled load to iron and fold. She pressed the steamer and sprayed a hot sizzle over naked cotton on the bench. She grabbed the corners and squared each sheet neat in the hot silence of the empty room.

It came and went, the pale light of a silent sorcery, the blood moon in her head, blond crystal that dappled crimson along the edge of her vision. She saw the shape of a legend, blue magic that wasn't destiny. But in those moments of inherent bloom she metamorphosed into flames. Burning that grew from a buzz or tingle, an aura or radiance whose curlicues a god of mist in the dead of a night aching with want might know. So she made paper boats from tea leaves, watched them sail at an altitude that improvised a prayer of love, sublimity and freedom growing bigger than distance yet lazing by her side at dusk.

Her desire for more filled the space between each chore. She shook off the imprint of her dreams, limericks that sailed her into clouds where she prowled the horizon and watched the world below take shape or fall apart. She waited for letters or the ring of a telephone, but her mother never wrote, let alone rang.

Jolainne scoured pots and pans, scrubbed sheets and floors. She flipped omelets and mackerel with butter on a tiny stove, plated them on gawky bread sold cheap for shape—the yeast's malice in uneven rise. The market's malevolence too: blue potatoes fresh all seasons, no small act of beauty, blessed anyhow. Finally, a note from Kinshasa, so brief it was just a telegram, but it wore her mother's childlike scrawl: *Your father is sick. Send money.*

Marie-Toure laughed it off. "Welfare isn't loaves and fishes. I live on government keep—where do I get sous for your mother?"

It was Mamadou who peeled out sous, pushed them into Jolainne's hand. "You're my favorite. Think of me as a honey father."

His deep belly laughter, as she blinked. She trusted a father's face. Unlike a mother's sharp one full of edges. A father's face was warm, soft-eyed and gave courage; Mamadou's was none of that. He wasn't the brown daddy she wanted near her babies, near anyone's babies.

She looked at his money.

"And me," said Auntie. "Give me some." The flesh in her arms swung.

Jolainne counted a few notes.

"No." Mamadou pushed back her hand. "Generosity will be the death of you."

Marie-Toure clicked her tongue. "What about my generosity?" She wagged a finger at Mamadou and his beard. "See how she's clever—the grades she gets in that école. Soon she'll go to collège and be a professeur. Already the girl is feeding a village."

"Do a good deed and throw it into the sea. Must you announce it?"

"A good deed is something one returns. Are you giving me money or what, Mamadou?"

"Easy," he said, and pulled a wad from his back pocket. He pinched out a third, rolled it and slipped it in Marie-Toure's bosom, right there between her plump breasts.

But his intense eyes shimmered on Jolainne's face, as she wondered about the generosity her auntie spoke of—perhaps the clothes, loads of them, from the second-hand shop.

"See? I told you," guffawed Marie-Toure. "We mesh."

Jolainne had no idea what Mamadou did for work. He was available all the time, like her, running eternal errands for her aunt. He closed her fist to make sure she kept her money, and the linger of his fingers told her he'd come to collect. He did. He had feelers for precisely when Marie-Toure heaved and waddled her way out of the shoebox flat, down all those flights of stairs.

Jolainne began sending money home often. Mamadou collected often. She ran between chores, hurrying north then south laundrying, cooking, sweeping, but outwardly she smiled. She played Auntie in the big man's arms when Auntie was off again, yet inside was the howl of grief drowning seedlings of hope, hopscotching for weeks and then months, years moving away. She sent money home but her father still died. His virus was one of poverty and a broken heart for his far-gone child donated as a migrant to distant lands.

She never got to see, even from a distance, the Tour Saint-Jacques, the Notre-Dame, the Arc de Triomphe de l'Étoile, or any château or galerie for that matter. Sometimes she saw fountains in a park. Though they had ruby-throated hummingbirds that reminded her of the motherland, none of those fountains was crystalline or pissing water high up into the sky. The perfumes Mamadou sometimes gifted her were cheap shit from some pharmacy nowhere near rue Scribe, rue Bachaumont or des Champs-Élysées. Sure, once or thrice Mamadou cracked open a bottle of bubbles, but Jolainne was lucky to get half a cup between chores, and only at Mamadou's insistence. Auntie gobbled the rest, it didn't matter how many notes of Grasse rose, jasmine grandiflorum, mandarine or patchouli floated from the fizz.

And Mamadou finally moved on—it broke Auntie. There was nothing for Jolainne but misery in the city of light. And Lubumbashi! Pro Bono! They couldn't even get her name.

Poetry shimmered into the vastness of Jolainne's lonesomeness. She ran and ran with her chores, verse in her head in bright patches until she lost count and collapsed in sleep.

He stares at her with those black velvet eyes. But they are half-sighted, fuzzy, waiting for her form to shape. There's turbulence in his blankness, confusion. The room and its tiny bed and cold, hard floor expand between them. The reality is firm: he's here. His crossed eyes wander to track her. She stands waiting. He focuses on her face. As his blurriness falls, his hand reaches out, or begs for a drink. But there's no herbed soup or soft red wine.

She reaches to touch him, falls back at his sudden movement, a snatching away as from a threat. His eyes begin to loll. His mouth forms and deforms, pulling words like bile from his gut. The yawn of his maw floats and shifts in a cloud, the skin on his face stretching and unstretching, black worms moving inside it. The spasm of his hands, reaching, and reaching. She presses against a wall—nowhere to go. His face pulls out, a second face, drifting towards her in its foggy form, grimaced in anger or anguish. His words are echoes vibrating the room, even as his double face folds back in and becomes one with itself.

His words get clearer with each try. Finally, she makes out what he's saying, "Arrêtez."

"Arrête de faire quoi?"

But he doesn't explain why or what he wants her to stop. Instead he says, "Mon Dieu." She looks at him in bafflement. "Je suis un ami," he says.

"Je suis aussi ton amie." She tries the important question: "Comment vous appelez-vous?"

He blinks. "Je m'appelle ..." He blinks, as if the words are lost.

"Comment vous appelez-vous, s'il vous plait," she begs for this name.

"S'il vous plait," he copies her words.

"Es-tu Alain? Divin? Rivlin? Yavan?"

"Mon Dieu," he says in his limited speech.

She notices his hair, long and slippery, not the tight curls he wore as a boy. And his skin—it's milk white.

She offers a hand. "Viens." Her words are a whisper, words from a novel she hasn't read. He takes her clutch, climbs to his feet. His rise is wonky. She puts both hands to steel him. He towers above her. His first walk is a totter. Is that her heart's whisper, or a sigh in her head? A rhythm in his form invites her to dance. But he's yet to walk, her little man all grown. She tries not to see his manhood. It's right there, taut as an oak. If he has thoughts at all, wonky after wonky step as he finds his feet, sex is the furthest thing.

He's perfect, imperfect. She's playing goddess. She has created a man in her own image, embossed in her memory. Now that she has him, she wonders, what will she do with him? How will he fit in her world? This locked-down world ridden with a plague. And right now, she has teaching to do, a virtual class of writing students waiting for her to log on. She did go to collège but she's not yet a professeur.

Now she has this one to teach. Her man. He's her man. Her lonesomeness across the years has been a curse. But now … She looks at him.

I look at her looking at me. Eyes into eyes. Hers, inquisitive. Mine? I don't know. Waiting, probably, if eyes can wait. What do I know? At this moment, so much, so little. I know this woman made me, that I should probably call her "Mother" or "Mama" or "Maman".

What I don't know is why she made me. Perhaps it's a mystery to her too. I hope not. I hope she has some idea of my role here, in her life. Behind her I see a wall, a door. There's often a wall and a door in a beginning. It must be a beginning. I am born. Created. I exist in time now, but not her time—at least not completely. I am the unborn born.

I've seen it happen, but it's my first time. I know much, I know nothing. The memories I have and carry from a past time: a continuous pulse, maybe a heart. A welcoming warmth. Shapes in the darkness of the friendly void, whispering, sometimes singing, always naming, some counting.

Counting what? I don't know. I don't remember. Same difference now. There are shapes, voices. Sometimes they send a smaller shape. They murmur, "You have been called," and that's it. She called me, this woman. I've no idea how. But I'm here, and that matters. Words come as natural as the wind, yet I've never experienced the wind. Or have I? I'm inside with the speech of outside.

So difficult now, to speak to the woman. Her world is complex.

She seems impatient, even as her fingers detail my body. I exist, she knows this. She's not happy, not frightened. Expecting, maybe, but I am already here. My memories are impossible. I can't define myself, except through "I", knowing it is and it isn't who I really am. The knowledge is too big. This place, this woman, her world.

I look at her. The stare has changed its owner. My reflection is in the black of her eyes. I am there, black on black. I know colors—how? I must learn. Everything. I am an apprentice. I'm willing.

I carry the strength of the sun, the subtlety of the wind, the solidity of water, the comfort of earth. I am a story. A gargoyle sleeping in a corner. I encompass all limits, offer no borders. I am here, between her hands. She created me, I created me.

When lightning hits a tree, the tree burns. But what made the lightning? What made the clouds the bolt escaped from? The story has so many beginnings, it has none. There are no promises between the created and the creator. Only experiences. Pieces that compose something.

A start is as good as any—and yet ... She began before me, and I before her. I remember, I forget. Each story has a price. It becomes your bones, your flesh, your laughter, your tears. We exchange vows through our held gaze. But is she ready? Is she really ready? For us.

She's waiting for me to say something, right now.

"Laisse-moi," I say, and close my eyes.

"Laisse-moi," he said, and closed his eyes. Leave me? Leave?

Jolainne's tears were not disappointment. For the first time in her life she understood rage. In a heartbeat, he was her mother. He was Marie-Toure. He was Mamadou. He was every urchin that had called her Lubumbashi. Pro Bono. If she had a bucket and a spade she would dig and bury him beyond reason. He was everything she dreamt about, and nothing close to its script. He was the sun that was a coalmine. The autumn that was a fog so dark and dirty she couldn't see her mind.

She looked at him: naked bum on her floor, knees up, head tucked in his elbows. She understood one thing more: he was unsure of his role. And she had nothing left to teach. Not for him, no. She had nothing. She spat on the floor. There'd be no standing ovation. Life had changed, things had moved on, and his story was a pestilent linger worse than the plague of her world. She hadn't marked the spot, but he would go back to the clay—whether he understood the words or not.

Spaces in the dust roads filled with reddish-brown wind—she wept for lost childhoods. And when it was over, she hoped there'd be clearer skies.

She sees her lost childhood, spaces filled with dust roads. She longs to see the shiny leaves of a tropical tree, wonders why no mango hit a head to save her.

A texture of shadows swirls with bifocals in the city library, blows its mist on new faux book spines blurred with mermaids and inky typeface. It will be gone by morning, changing minds about justice. Fe-fi-fo-fum: luring everything but text to clouds and oceans, photographing smudges and spreads. Natural history pollution to the moon and back captured on phone. The sky might fall.

Her pen is poised to write a story that interrupts itself in lambent colors that don't match as they flicker between moments. If she could hide in poems, she'd scribe no apology or complaint, just a dirge (not a fête) of words that keep going. That's enough. Alain, Divin, Rivlin, Yavan is gone. She wants no compassion—half-smiled or whole. Just a corridor she can borrow for a reference to feel included more than a minute and forty seconds more more, and not in a second-hand shop. STOP. More more.

THE WIDOW'S ROOSTER

THE SUN grew faint. It disappeared. The wail of a horn entered the horizon and fell to the dirt. Villagers tumbled from their huts. They swept into the black night and raced towards the sound.

They reached a clearing by the river cutting through the hillocks, into a glade kindled with flames. The eyes of owls perched on baobab trees alongside the shore silently observed.

Dawa the medicine man gleamed with animal fat. He gyrated around flames, sisal skirt swishing, cowry shells jingling on arms and feet. War paint on his face.

Villagers shrank from his cursing bone.

A figure wrapped in a sheet, his head scattered with ash, pushed to the fore. "What's this?"

The medicine man stopped and glared. "A terrible deed has happened."

Foretelling a story, villagers arranged themselves on logs. Others crouched or sat on red dirt. A flock of restless shadows in the low canopy as vultures landed.

"See? A warning of death that'll happen if this crime isn't fixed. One of you," Dawa stared sternly, "has eaten old woman Ndebe's rooster!"

"What?" Lament trembled in the throng.

"Who!"

A woman spat on the ground. "Ceaseless wonders."

"As you know," continued Dawa. "Old woman Ndebe is a widow.

Her husband Ngosi was a good man. But he died poor—that's what happens when you listen to a woman and take your daughters to school instead of marrying them for cows."

The crowd heckled.

"Where are the daughters now? In the city with cowless husbands they chose. And their poor mother? Fending for herself in a barren piece of land."

He scowled.

"I loaned my good-for-nothing son to help the widow. From dust to sundown he was to cut wood, fetch water and bring fish from the river. The lazy no good could only manage twigs and tadpoles. Many times —" He shook his head. "I was tempted to use juju to right that boy! But the ancestors wouldn't allow it. A medicine man doesn't heal himself or his family."

"You woke us from our wives to —" began the ash-headed man with a sheet.

Dawa's hand silenced him. "One of you had the audacity to eat this poor woman's one and only rooster!"

"If the cockerel is missing, maybe a wild dog took it."

"Or a hyena," another suggested.

"Wisdom doesn't come overnight!" barked the medicine man. "The only hyena that ate old woman Ndebe's rooster is standing on two legs and wearing the face of a man."

"Why can't it be a woman?" asked the ash-headed man.

"Old man of the village," said Dawa. "You're give shade like a baobab tree. But you speak like a fool. A woman has no brains, but she has a heart. She'll not snatch the last morsel from a widow's mouth. This deed —" He pulled out a bag of wet feathers and cooked bones. Hurled them at the crowd. "This is the work of a man."

"Ayah!" Outrage.

"The poor widow's cockerel!"

"What thief is too lazy to bury bones? He cooked the rooster in the widow's own stone hearth. Ate and spat the bones in her own kitchen."

"Have mercy!"

"The poor woman collapsed in grief," said Dawa. "So I say to the fool who did this. Come forward. Repent and I'll cast my bones and chase away bad spirits. You'll repay the widow with a spotless chicken, and all will be forgotten."

Nobody moved.

"I'll point my bone!" He looked around. "Very well. I have no choice."

The crowd squealed and collapsed as the medicine man pointed. A sharp breeze swept through the fuggy night. Suddenly, a cry in the gathering's belly. People scattered.

Dawa marched into the parting. Right there, convulsing on the ground, lay his own son.

"What's this?"

"Sloth, that's what," said the woman who spat.

Dawa sprang at the boy, shook him. "Quickly, what's this?!"

The one who spat spoke. "Let me tell you the wisdom of a woman. That slothful imbecile of yours didn't want to wake up, that's what. Ask him."

"True … father," gasped the boy in his dying breath. "Every … day … before dawn … the stupid … rooster … crowed!"

RAIN DOESN'T FALL ON ONE ROOF

MAWE! Her girl self calls out to the mango-scented comfort of her mother. She reaches for the clouds, tiny fingers aching for a long ago touch.

An alarm goes off in the dimly lit room, curtains drawn. Bapoto, twenty-eight, stirs in the bed. Her cornrows are disheveled. The alarm blasts out again, yanking her from the unworldliness of her dream. Some nights, she could swear … her mother's soft breath on her brow. Other nights, just the coldness of absence. Mawe hangs over the bed, all eyes, mute. Holding in her arms, in monochrome, baby Bapoto curious about the world.

Bapoto groans. She rubs her eyes, gropes for the clock on a bedside table. The alarm goes off again, its disturbance like her name. Bapoto —it means "noise". What was wrong with Blessing? Or Bohlale—it means "wisdom". Why did she have to get a name full of turbulence? *The name of your great-grandmother*, explained Mawe. *It's in the clan, your turn came*. But why? little Bapoto had cried. *We carry our ancestors*, said Mawe.

Bapoto hurls the squealing device to silence on the ground. She leaps out of bed. Retrieves the clock, restores it on her dresser. Reaches to flick on bathroom lights as she shrugs out of African-print pajama pants, a snake goddess slithering in the savannah, neck to heel.

Bapoto enters the living room, rubs her hair briskly with a towel. She's wearing an ebony t-shirt and a wrap skirt. No makeup. She wraps the towel around her head, sits by the computer. Turns the power on.

"Come on, come on!"

She logs into her email account.

Nothing from the recruitment agency.

"These guys for real?"

She logs into online banking, accounts view. $17.50 sits between her and poverty. No money to send back home, even if she wanted to. She looks at a pile of unpaid bills under the dining table. Gasps as she remembers Lochie's music class invoice.

A framed portrait sits on the wall next to Bapoto. She is wearing a blissful face and a graduation gown. A scholarship—her legs from the motherland to this world.

Mawe gruff-gruffed her laughter over the telephone, the deep belly sound of a lioness delighted with her cub. It persuaded Bapoto into a masters course.

"Lochie?"

Bapoto opens the door to Lochie's room from the corridor.

"Lochie!" louder. She peers into the room. A diminutive bump beneath the bedcover betrays her son's presence.

Bapoto strides into the room, yanks away the covers. "Lochland Boitumelo Piers."

"I don't like Boitumelo." His voice is muffled, full of sleep.

"It means 'joy'. Where you come from is important. Lochie. Lochie?"

Silence.

"Lochie, are you dead?"

"Yes."

He's lying facedown, the back of his head a riot of curls. Not as tight as Bapoto's kinky hair unwoven; his is the elastic hair of mixed race.

"We'll be late for school, darling. You need to wake up now." Lochie doesn't stir. "I said NOW."

Lochie, seven years old, turns, big chocolate eyes looking at Bapoto. "Are you cross, Mamma?"

"Not yet. But I will be if you don't hurry." She ruffles his curls as he slips out of bed. He's fragile looking. Bapoto follows closely behind as he heads for the bathroom.

"Mamma!" He shuts the door against her face.

"Don't forget to brush your new teeth—remember what the dentist said." Bapoto talks to him across the door. "You don't want those pulled out because they're rotting."

"They won't rot." Mouth busy with brushing.

"You've got music today?"

Lochie grunts acknowledgement. "Teacher said we've got to pay the invoice."

Bapoto's face falls. "Pay today?"

"Or no music class."

Bapoto turns on the kettle. A gentle purr as water begins to boil. She sits the tea bag in her moonlight mug.

She pulls a bowl of leftover mash and chicken schnitzel from the fridge. Prises open the container's lid and drops it in the sink. She puts the bowl in the microwave, slams the door shut and presses *Dish Warmer*.

The kettle's hum is louder. Now it begins to shake and will soon turn itself off. The water has boiled. She makes her tea as she likes it—lots of milk, then one minute in the microwave to add heat.

She packs Lochie's food in the lunchbox, trimly arranges in a separate container an apple, yoghurt (the squeeze-me kind), one fruit bar, one cereal bar and an umbrella lolly. Cherry flavor. He likes that. He doesn't know the lusciousness of fresh mango plucked from a tree. The aroma of durian miles out.

She glances at the kitchen door. "You coming out of the bathroom, buddy, or what?" Silence. "Lochie! Are you done?"

"I'm done, Mamma." He answers from somewhere.

"Put your clothes on now. Quick."

He enters the kitchen in his school uniform.

"Why do you always have to say 'quick', Mamma?"

"Because you need to hurry. Did you wash sleep from your eyes?"

"Y-yes."

"Cleaned your teeth the ..."

"The way the dentist said, yes!"

"Don't speak to me that way."

"What way?"

"Just dress up and eat your breakfast." Bapoto sips her tea. "Remember you gave me this mug last Mother's Day?"

"Me?"

"Course you, silly. From the school stall."

"What's for breakfast?" he asks.

Bapoto nods at the table. "You know what's breakfast."

"I don't like baked beans on toast."

"Since when?" Her voice is distracted. She reaches, straightens his shirt collar.

"Aww."

"Don't be silly—that doesn't hurt." She combs his curls with her fingers.

"Aww!"

"Stop wriggling, Lochie. I said STOP. That doesn't hurt either."

"Let me do it to you and see if it doesn't hurt."

"Stop being silly! I mean it."

"You're being silly."

Slap!

Her strike on his cheek is not vicious, just enough to silence. He looks at her, bewildered. She has never hit him before. His hand rises to the cheek.

Bapoto stares at her son. Then she looks aghast at the palm that struck him. They stand like that, frozen a moment. Bapoto's hand flies to her mouth, too late to stop a wretched sob.

She reaches and cradles Lochie's head to her bosom. But he pulls away. She tries again: "My honey."

Lochie backs out of reach.

Bapoto lurches towards the bathroom. With another sob, she locks herself in. Her shoulders shake, her chest is heaving. A migrant alone in this world, far from her clan. But they rely on her—she sends money when she can, to support the rest. She feels overwhelmed. She puts a hand to her throat, strangles sound from reaching her lips.

Mawe was wisdom; she would not have reacted so sharply to a youngun.

Patience mothers a beautiful child, she used to say. So why can't Bapoto go the same way in training her son? *We carry our ancestors.* Bapoto is afraid: how much of Mawe is left within? Bapoto has lost tradition. She has lost language—the chain broke with Lochie.

She runs the tap to muffle her crying. Now she's ransacking the medicine cabinet. Small bottles and boxlets of medicine crash to the floor. She finds a bottle of tablets, empties the pills onto her palm.

"Useless. Useless. I'm good for nothing."

She lifts the pills towards her mouth. Her hand trembles.

A scratch on the door.

Bapoto's hand lowers. She faces the door.

"Lochie?" softly. Silence. "Honey, is that you?" Silence.

She leans down to look, sees a shadow moving on the other side of the door.

"Lochie," even softer. "I know you're there …"

She goes on all fours, looks underneath the doorway, but Lochie is gone. With a cry, Bapoto hurls the pills and empty bottle to the floor, and sobs into her hands.

Anger does not cook yams, says Mawe in her head.

Bapoto pulls herself together. Opens the door. Lochie is standing, dustpan and broom in hand. Silently, they tidy the mess—scattered pills and broken glass.

Bapoto turns on the kettle in the kitchen. Lochie butters their toast. His quiet warmth patches her fragility.

"Eat your breakfast." She doesn't know what else to say. She watches as he gobbles his toast. He's seeking to please her. He catches her gaze and smiles. It's hesitant, pleading reassurance. She ruffles his curls, sweeps him into a hug. "I love you, kiddo."

"Love you too, Mamma."

"Sorry I was cross before. Got things on my mind."

They race to catch the train.

Lochie is doing a cowboy stride as they approach the school gate. "Look, Mamma," he says, strutting. He puts a hand to the waistband of his shorts, yanks out an invisible gun. "Boom! Boom!" His other hand cracks an equally invisible whip to the ground. "Phew! Phew!"

"You make a cool warrior."

"It's Indiana Jones." Pause. "I get cranky pants too."

"Really?"

"When I'm hungry."

"Then I'm glad you ate your toast."

A little boy in the schoolyard is bouncing a big red ball on the basketball court. Bounce. Bounce. Bounce. He aims at the net, his arms and body bobbing to a silent countdown: three, two, one. He goes for the shot. Misses.

"Isn't that Josh? Go play with him, Lochie. I'll watch you until the bell rings."

He dumps his schoolbag at her feet and races off full throttle.

Her reaction with Lochie this morning, and that stint in the bathroom, it all deeply troubles.

Back home, she slips off the crochet wrap top and plaid skirt she wore to drop Lochie, anything to look like a decent mum. She pulls on the t-shirt, wraps a skirt. Without a job and a padlock on her mood swings, she doesn't feel decent. Or a good mum. What she is, is a stranger.

She checks her mobile phone. No text message from Bill.

"Billy-Be-Childish," she says out loud and laughs to herself. Bill is surplus work. Her new flame after the divorce. Last time they went out, he got so drunk he puked. She held his head as he retched his guts into a sober toilet that gurgled. Gurgle, gurgle. Despite her help, he couldn't aim straight. Showers of orange all over the floor resembled salmon roe. It was a goo-soaked head that lifted from the bowl.

She checks her email. No news from the job agency on results of the interview with Zodiac Insurance. She's gently been probing on email and would like a definite response: yes or no. Who cares? Darn it, she cares. They would phone, not email, if she got the job. But no one from the agency has phoned since the interview. Aren't there any more jobs in the city? Or perhaps the agency has given up on her.

A wave of despondency engulfs her. Yesterday Lochie told her about his friend Nick who cried all through music class.

"Why did he cry?" she asked.

"Because he couldn't play his guitar."

"Doesn't he know how to play?"

"He does but the teacher wouldn't let him."

"Why not? It was music class."

"His dad was going to pay but he forgot. So Teacher said Nick had to leave music class."

"Did you feel bad for Nick?"

"Y-yeah."

And Bapoto knew she would pay Lochie's music invoice if it killed her.

Bill phones early afternoon.

"Hey, babes."

"Hello, you. What's going on?"

"Work's going on. I'm busy."

"Want to do dinner?"

"Have you got a babysitter for Lochie Locks?"

"He hates it when you call him that."

"So have you got a sitter?"

"You know I can't afford one. Come have dinner with us."

"Not tonight, babes."

"Tomorrow night?"

"Can't tomorrow."

"Any time soon?"

"Don't know, babes. Maybe Friday. I've got this client proposal. Got to finish it and clinch the deal, you know."

"Yes," she says. But she doesn't know.

"I'd better get back to work, babes."

"Of course."

She throws a tie-front cardigan over the t-shirt, grabs the house keys and goes for a walk. A quiet calm surrounds the botanical gardens. She walks briskly between trees and the shadows they cast, looking for spots of sun and the feel of its rays on her skin. The sun is coy. Like an elusive lover, she comes and goes.

Bapoto sits on a grass-green bench by a pond and watches silver swans glide on the soiled water. She wishes Mawe had less fear of a plane: *My bones are old for aeroplaney, hey*. Mawe would have seen a little beauty in this foreignness. The swans float across, tranquil as Mawe. If only Bapoto's life were half as graceful … She imagines herself wearing a leopard leotard, moving in a slow dance to a soaring melody in a room full of mirrors. She is happy, ever so happy in that image.

Why is her life so full of clouds now? The past two weeks have been the worst. After two job interviews with the bank, and seven psychometric tests (seven!), the agency phoned to say it was close. Close? she thinks angrily. Who wants to be runner-up in an interview if it doesn't get you the job?

She talked to Bill about it, asked what he thought about Bapoto calling the bank for results of the psychometric tests.

"I wouldn't do that if I were strapped to explosives," Bill said.

"What if the explosives were a miniature kind and strapped to your gonads?" snapped Bapoto.

The human resources girl at the bank was far more heartening than Bill. She didn't sound like the man at the interview, the one with the face of a warthog. Bapoto recalls that man very clearly, how he sat at the panel, looking at her as if she wore two heads.

"In the language reasoning test," the human resources girl said, "you scored thirty-seven, where the average percentile is thirty-one. Results show that you are a good communicator, articulate and with sound vocabulary.

"In the numeric reasoning test, you scored thirty-four, where the average percentile is also thirty-one. Results show 100 per cent accuracy in the questions you attempted, with strong computational and analytical ability.

"In the abstract reasoning test, you scored thirty-six, where the average percentile is again thirty-one …"

A strategic thinker, honest and fair, emotionally calm … Overall, thought Bapoto, she was perfect for the stupid bank.

That night of the knowing, that she was good but not good enough for these people, Bapoto had knelt under the framed photo in her bedroom, cried to the spirit of Mawe, asking if perhaps it was a curse. Because she had broken family, lost language.

For the first time, Mawe didn't answer.

Lochie surges into her arms. He's chatty all the way nonstop, always like this after school.

"Teacher was okay about music class."

"Really?"

"Kyle brought a tadpole, got sent to the principal's office."

"That's rough."

"Nick says a man in Crichton was eaten by his lizards."

"My word!"

"He had hundreds of lizards as pets. Hundreds!"

"Golly gosh."

"Do you know what lizards do, Mamma? They're like snakes."

"But they have legs. How are they like snakes?"

"First they poison you. And when you die or get subsconscious …"

"Unconscious, honey."

"When you die or are unconscious, they eat you."

"Not nice."

"They ate up all his face, Mamma."

"I've got a story too. This guy in the US had fifty-six wild pets."

"Wild?"

"Lions, cougars, pumas … fifty-six, can you believe it? Was he nuts or what?"

"Is he dead like the man with the lizards?"

"Dead, yes."

"Did the animals kill and eat him up?"

"No, doctors found a bullet wound."

"The animals didn't shoot him."

"No, honey, they didn't. He put a Colt 45 to his head …" She illustrates with two pointy fingers to Lochie's temple. "And fired."

"Why would anyone do that?"

"He …" She stops. Her throat is suddenly tight. "Um … well … He owed money."

"To a lot of people?"

"I, I think … yes."

She remembers the sadness that hit like an arrow. Its poisoned tip pierced her denial of death and its muteness. But dying is not silence. Mawe speaks to Bapoto all the time.

Dinner is chicken schnitzel and mash again. Bapoto thinks of corn meal and spiced peanut sauce. Firewood-grilled tilapia, all skin head to tail. You eat it from the head down, never tail up. Lochie wolfs his plate like a famished jackal. They play chess and he whops her—she's bad at it and he knows. It's the only thing Bapoto is not good at. Well, that and getting employment.

"Snooze time, super champ," she says.

"Not yet …" he grumbles.

She gives him a little tickle on his toes. "Yes yet … off you go."

"Do I have to?"

"You need the sleep of a thousand men."

"Why?"

"So you can grow, silly."

"You're just making that up, Mamma."

"Never. All right then, buster," she puts on a singsong voice. "Goodnight." She unfolds his hands from her waist.

"Kiss?"

"Ab-so-lutely. Love you, honey."

"I love you too, Mamma."

Despite the lightness of her tone, she's exhausted. It feels like the end of the longest imaginable day. Her head sinks into her hands. It's heavy, as if filled with dark gray clouds cascading and churning and threatening to explode everything about her. How long is her financial situation going to stay this rough?

Her phone hums with a text message from Bill: "Headache. Shit. I'm stuffed. Had a shit-arsed day."

"Sorry to hear that," she texts back. "What are you doing now?"

He phones. "I'm watching a doco on satellite telly."

"What's the documentary about?"

"Share market stuff. Heck's wrong with this remote?"

"Bill, I don't know what's wrong with your remote."

"What the hell …?!"

She imagines him planted in front of the television like a vegetable, his coarse hands fluffing about with the remote. Soon he'll begin to sprout.

She wonders what she sees in him. At first his rustic charm and quirkiness were cute. Different from the city knob-heads she was dating. Lochie's father was not her first wretched spell. She's never been lucky with men. But she waited for Mawe's passing before she left the bad marriage, unable to face her mother's disappointment—*It's your cross,* Mawe would say about the situation, when Bapoto hinted at unsettlement over the phone. *He's your new family now. You don't break family.*

She realizes Bill is saying something on the other end of the line.

"What was that again, hun?" she asks.

"Said I can't do Friday."

Billy-Be-Childish. Bapoto refuses to think about him after she hangs up. It wasn't that hard after all, breaking up with a lump of clay. For all Mawe's tolerance, she would have seen Bill as hyena poop that reeked, no matter how tiny.

Bapoto turns on the laptop and logs into her online university course. The computer hums, freezes twice, and she has to restart it. She is close to tears as the machine reboots. She can't afford to replace the darn thing.

Back online, she navigates to the higher education bulletin board. She sees the unit convenor's announcement—results of the last unit are out. She clicks the *My Grades* toolkit and mentally works out her score: twenty-eight out of thirty in coursework, sixty-six point five out of seventy in the final assignment … She blinks, blinks again and belts out a hoot. Ninety-four point five per cent! That's a high distinction. "Your contributions were incisive and thoughtful," her tutor says in the comments.

"Tell that to the job market," Bapoto says wryly.

Fight with courage, my child. Never with anger, or despair.

A fruity smell envelops her. It's like a pineapple or a melon, but she knows it's a mango. Because she can taste it: a moist sourness wrapped in sweet fragrance. And Mawe's words, a fragile murmur, waft in and out of her head: *Rain … rain … falls … falls … on many roofs … roofs.*

Lochie's snores, more like purrs, in the adjacent room climb and fall like ocean waves. Such softness for such strength. That boy is her metal. The silver in her clouds. Suddenly, she feels rejuvenated.

Before she logs off the computer, she checks her mailbox. A new email from the job agency titled "FW: Your recent application for *position of (Ref. no: 002VWP)*" has an attachment.

Bapoto clicks the email to open it.

DANGED BLACK THING

(WITH E. DON HARPE)

"DEY'S A TIME TO MAKE a stand, and dey's a time to make tracks," my daddy used to say. I didn't understand what he meant, 'cause I'd never had to do either, but the fact is, I'm a right smart gal. I took one look at the yard filled with them danged gizmos and just about hit the road.

My name is Champ McPherson, and I've seen hardware and software do all shit. Viruses wiping more than one system clean, and I never had the inclination to get the hell out of dodge. But you don't have to tell me twice. One look out the front window, and out the back door I leapt.

The first of them danged black thangs arrived at noon. I watched them from the safety of the attic (locked), knew the electric fence would do a number on them. And it did! At first! But soon the fence lay on the ground smoking, as they rattled bolts, banged at the chain link, jumped back and forth, all angry and riled, getting ready to rush the house, looking to gain entrance by breaking down doors or smashing windows. They were fine-looking portables, laptops mostly, but from the attic window I could make out a few palmtops, desktops and a couple of mainframes chugging up steam down below. Every one of them black as ebony.

The mainframes lent muscle to the rest of the apparatus down there and, before long, they'd smash into the house. I knew.

• • •

Wasn't she something? I found her at an ancient shop in Omega Street one mild autumn day. "Second hand," the shopgirl said. "Some missionaries from Mozambique. Didn't want a dollar for it, but I gotta make a buck."

I eyed the machine in astonishment, ran my fingers across her dark silk coat. I stroked the feminine outline of her screen, the contours of which bore the silhouette of a black woman's face, lush lips, eyes like a deer's and all. She was perfect. Just the thing I needed to zing up Slade's humdrum life. 'Twas hard enough getting his notice in bed; a piece of equipment might spark more attention off him, I thought. He could use her as a journal or a word processor, perhaps a platform upon which to test the Tec-build software for his shuttles.

Slade, he was a good boy, played it straight. Head full of tick-tock thoughts, I could read him like a watch, ever since and before we wed. He was a shuttle repairman down the South Depo. Every day he worked an eight-to-five. I never once knew him to miss a day of work, not even an hour. Soon as he was done at the factory, he'd be home like clockwork, never skipped the evening news.

Slade, he lit up like a Christmas tree, soon as his eyes set on the notebook.

"Her name's Embu," I said. "Bought her just fer yew."

"Yews de sweetest thang, my white chocolate," he said to me. "Brought me a dark truffle." He at once powered the machine. Her screen saver had cocoa eyes full of soul and thick braided hair, all kinky. Her skin was black velvet.

"She looks almost human," he said in stupefaction.

"Shock proof," I said. "Trendy, ain't she? Packs a refined graphics interface. Real time tracker too. Inbuilt. Yew can never lose her."

Puppy eyes sought consent or authentication that he could fiddle with his new toy.

"Go on." I smiled.

He vanished into the study, and I capped the occasion by cooking for him. It was an old gourmet recipe I got from my grandma, back in '17 before she passed.

I grabbed a couple cans of red beans and a box of instant rice from a shelf in the pantry, took a pound or so of hot sausage, some okra from the chill bin, didn't take long for the kitchen to start smelling like the old South, back when there still was an old South. A random thought crossed my mind as I set the table. Before I knew it, I had spiked a punch to set the mood right.

Slade emerged from his den with an odd look, gobbled dinner in silence. Soon as I rose to clear plates, he gripped my arm, escorted me to our chamber. There, he lay with me with more zeal than I had ever witnessed, with more ardor than he'd ever shown, even on a mating moon.

From an eight-to-five, Slade became a nine-to-four, never mind it sliced our income. He left for work an hour late, having spent time with Embu; left the assembly line an hour early, another session with the machine before the evening news. His eyes now carried more than their pensive light. What went on inside them was more than tick-tock thoughts.

As for Embu, when I wiped her screen, her eyes were nicely smoked up, her brow smudged with color, her ebony cheeks spread with scarlet blush to lift her complexion even more. Her braided hair was kinkier than ever, her full lips blood keen.

"Oh my," I said to her with a tart smile. "Aren't yew just de most darling little thang? Africa is where yew belong. Wilderness camp or an elephant graveyard some place in Mozambique. Don't know as I've ever seen a cuter ... notebook, and I reckon Slade—well, *honey*, he thinks so too!"

A leopard-patterned petticoat, the shape of a rose, spattered with dark rosettes, glided along a velvet thigh across the screen. But what got to me was the smile, Embu's teeth like freshwater pearls. I reached for the machine with spiteful hands, ready to crash her to the floor and trample her good. And I caught myself. Surely! This was a tad paranoid to say the least, perhaps even a smidgen over the frame. Was my mind hot and bothered with jealousy of a laptop?

There was no necessity for it, for sure, as Slade took me now each night, mating moon or not. I had something solid with him; nothing could beat that. No stupid Tec-build would take my Slade away.

He still spent a lot of time in his den before the taking, so one day I had to know.

"Dis ain't right," I said to Slade. "What yew do in dere? What take so long? Yew know, wit Embu? What yew doing wit dat machine?"

"Stuff, just stuff. Nothing much."

"What kinda stuff?"

"A bit a dis, a bit a dat. Nothing much."

I raised an eyebrow, stared at him.

"Dat's de truth, yes, love," without flinch he said.

But with Embu's gilded brightness lighting up the house, I was certain that no spiked punch or dinner thing, not even Slade's need for me, fit the math to make him that committed, so aberrantly savage when we were joined between the sheets, when straight from the den he took me like a demon.

He kept coming back for more but, desolate, I understood. It was nothing to do with a statement that I was unresistingly scrumptious, and everything to do with Embu, wrapping my husband with the silk of her web.

One night, after yet another of my grandma's old-fashioned New Orleans dinners, he set out as usual for the den where Embu waited. I cleared the table, packed the dishes in the spinner, set it on. By the time the dishes were done and sparkling, Slade had still not emerged. I made myself a cuppa, steaming black coffee, laced it with the last of a bottle of brandy. I cupped the china with both hands, as if holding a fragile heart, finished my coffee alone.

Only then did I give up on Slade and, with it, any hope of a tumble. I thought I heard voices behind the door of the den, one crafty and eager, the other soft and caressing. Sounds like jungle, the mews and purrs of a leopard, the laughter of a hyena. I stood outside that door, hugged myself not for warmth but dread. Was what I heard a sound card processing inside a machine, or demons in the core of my head? With profound wretchedness and legs knock-kneed with sadness, I made my way to the chamber.

Slade ... He stole inside the sheets beside me as the clock inched towards midnight. I counterfeited sleep but he did not nudge me to wake me. I opened an eyelid, and there was no keen look on his face, the one he wore before he dragged me into his arms at dusk. Slade lay on his side, elbow under his head, half a smile on his face. He was fast asleep. He did not want me tonight; it hit me hard as he snored away. My husband did not want me.

Next evening, I cooked for him something different. I grabbed a couple of green onions from the pantry, tossed them on top of reserve marinade chicken in a ceramic dish, spooned in some olive oil and pepper, baked everything until golden. He wolfed without notice and vanished into the den.

He was even later coming to bed that night. I tossed and turned, tossed and turned again. Close to midnight, the door squealed, and he slunk into the bedroom. I sat up with riot hair, snapped on the bedside lamp.

There he stood, guilty as sin. He started to explain, something about some project or other. But I saw a hickey on his neck.

"Love at first bite, was it?"

Anger, when it arrived, came fast and hard like a thunderbolt. I leapt, cross-eyed with fury. My fist brushed past his jaw when I meant to punch his nose. I reached for his neck, proposing to strangle him, found it was sticky. I leant close, and a sickly aroma of maple syrup wafted into my nostrils. Maple! That hickey was no lean bite, no mistake: it was a premier hickey, no holdback on it. And Slade had smeared maple syrup on his neck for it. A leopard can't change its spots, and Embu was a wild one.

Finally, worn with hitting him, I lay on the bed and pondered slitting my wrists or shredding up Slade. But all I wanted to do really, I finally figured, was to shove effin Embu up his butt. The bubbles of something unformed spread inside me and rose to the surface but, before they could formulate into a plan, they were gone from my head.

This was real, how easy, a Zulu goddamn machine had replaced me.

Sobbing into my hands, I fled. Dressed in nothing but a negligee, I ran out of the bedroom, leapt down the steps and out the front door into a well-lit street.

Slade stamped at my heels in bedroom slippers. He was beside himself, saying over and over: "It was just stuff. Nothing much. Dat's de truth. Dat's de truth!" His feet closed fast. "Yew git back here. Champ McPherson."

I turned right, ran all the way to the freeway. There, right there in the middle of the road, I lay face up, arms spread.

And though the road was dead at night and no traffic haunted it, Slade beseeched me, "I love yew. Yews de sweetest thang. Git off de road!"

Just then, headlights rose from the distance. The red grew bigger and sharper until a turbo bus rolled into view. The driver was bobbin his head, lips pushed out like he was whistling.

Deaf to the rumble of the bus or Slade's pleading I lay silent. It took some time before I realized that Slade had stopped the bus; that the driver had raised me and tossed me onto grass at the other side of the road; that Slade had pulled me up by the arm and was leading me home.

Back in the house, I made straight for the den. But, again, Slade tried to calm me.

"Damn yew!" My fists pounded his face. I struggled with him, and was unstoppable this time. When I burst into the den, I was yelling and crying. I took hold of Embu, who sat grinning on his desk. She shuddered mildly, it seemed, as I raised her above my head and bashed her onto the ground. But her screen flew open and her face grew full of sweetness and deep secrets: a vague, butter smile full of knowing, the smile of an adulteress. I flung her against the wall, and she crashed back to the floor. I was falling and kicking and sweating and thrashing. I meant to wreck her once and for all. But when I was done, she shone darker and brighter than ever, finer than new.

Embu was shock proof.

Now she regarded me with a half-crooked smile. I moaned into the arm of my nightie that was torn and falling off my shoulder. I went down on all fours and cried to the gods of all ancestors when I wasn't cussing Slade.

"Godsake, Slade, a hickey!"

He drew me gently but firmly away from his den.

When he was asleep, I snuck out of the chamber and staggered right back to the den. I pushed Embu into a plastic bag and stashed her out with the garbage. Splendid thing there was a collection at dawn.

I slept until the wheels of the garbage truck woke me.

I found Slade in the kitchen, his arms tenderly wrapped around

Embu. He wore the defiant look of a boy protecting his toy. Her inbuilt tracking device had led him to her. He locked the den and put a security code on it.

Soon as he left for work, I ran out the garden and into the shed. I grabbed a hammer, beat down the door. I threw Embu into the trunk and sped all the way to the lake. Three big sways, *hooray!* and Embu pitched straight up into the air and down in an arch. She met the lake with a splash. Water closed over her head, and she did not come up.

I was bone weary when I arrived home. But elated I had got rid of that black bitch once and for all. I poured myself a cup of coffee, laced it with new brandy.

I was on a second cup when the danged gizmos arrived. Machines from hell, they were, Embu's spirits come to get me. Before I hit the back door to the nearest telebooth, where I could call the military, get smoke, bazookas and lasers on them, I looked out the attic window at a mainframe, a large male autobot, bulk iron and face like Shaka Zulu, an intel warrior most lustrous and robust. I thought how fine-looking a specimen … If Slade could do it, that selfish prick, heck! maybe I could.

But what I could do most with now was a plan to seduce a hunk in the middle of a riot.

DE TURTLE O' HADES

(WITH E. DON HARPE)

L*ike every African dictator, he was confusion's masterpiece*
—The Telegraph (August 2003)

ONE CLOUDY NOON in late October, a turtle moseyed past the edge of the Great Swamp and down a mud-cloaked road. He dawdled past rows of trees whose roots the bayou fed living organisms. Here, waters thickened to the color and texture of sunburnt porridge. Not much of the world had altered since the turtle's hibernation.

Except the diamond trees looked wild as ever and the Jacobean shrubs more rare and serene despite tepid southbound winds that rocked the murky waters. These same winds bore a depraved spirit that made blowflies lose their minds and brought with them the tale of the ashy monster of the bayou—the one that made a toy of the boogieman.

The turtle passed a timber plaque on the way, a sign that led towards—or perhaps had been—Sammy's Chicken Bar and Fried Green Tomatoes. By then, in this part of the swamp, wind had changed and lost its teasing. Now its mood matched that of the rest of the bayou, close to bog land. Tide swept in from the bayou's spirit to slap a coast ravenous for wandering smallies like the two fun-loving girls and a happy dog it had once swallowed whole. The smell was cavernous and green weedy, and it held more than a hint of fish.

The turtle waddled to a ramshackle hut, a single-room cabin that stood feet from the lip of the bayou. It had seen finer days, and was over seventy years old. No fit home for man or beast, someone lived there.

The turtle navigated three steps, seven splinters and nine cracks. Finally! He poked his head past a door, peered into the half-lit room, and found chaos and dereliction. And behold, there was the Man. He half-sat, half-slouched on a rocker, a bottle of booze in his hand. The turtle ambled deep into a smell of cabbages or was it feet?

They eyed each other.

The Man spoke first. "Yew want a drank o' this moonshine?"

"Ain't no moonshine fer me," said the turtle.

"Well. Ain't got no bourbon fer yew, or any o' dat fine liquor."

"All dat's none o' my thang," said the turtle.

"Ah be danged to know yore thang. What's yore name, turtle?" the Man said. "Ole Andy wants to know yore name."

"If yore name's Ole Andy, ah ain't no turtle."

"Who might ah be den, turtle?"

"Who yew are ain't who yew used to be. Call yerself Ole Andy, er something else. Call yerself whatever yew need to. Feel dem jitters slipping up on yew?"

"Ain't got no jitters. What yew say yore name is, turtle?"

"My name is Doc, don't yew go calling me turtle. Most folks just calls me Doc."

"Doc, huh," Ole Andy said. "Where yew from, Mister Doc Green Turtle?"

"Ovah in de black water. Born and bred ovah dere. Used to have a fambily ovah dere, but dey's all gone. Most o' dem is turtle soup now, else dey's grounded up fer one er de udder o' Miz Marie's potions."

"Did yew come here fer something, Doc, to tell Ole Andy something mabbe. Er just to discuss how cruel life has been fer yore fambily?"

"Ah gots something to tell yew, all right, dat's a fact. But ah don't know as how yew is ready just yet fer to hear de news. Might just strike yew down where yew's standing."

"Now dat we's all agreed on yore name, Doc Turtle, what might you be thunking about mine? My true identity?"

Doc Turtle did not reply. He did a crawl around the potbellied stove that the Man used to ward off October evening chill at dark. He wondered how a man once so potent could live in such squalor.

"Dis ole house," he wondered aloud those thoughts. "Dis house in Louisiana, she a whole lot different from what yew is used to, ain't she?" A couch, its hide worn out and faded, rested its back against the wall. Beside it, a scarred wooden table sufficient for the Man to take his meals. "Yew been chowing on cabbage?"

"Danged right—cabbage. Yew got something fancy fer me, like turtle soup mabbe?"

The turtle smiled. He peered around the stove and saw a grimed and cracked old mirror hung on one wall, a hotplate set on a sideboard by the wall; aside from them and the rocker the old man sat in, no other furnishings claimed space.

"Ain't she a lot different?" Doc Turtle looked at Ole Andy.

"Dat she is, bro, dat she is. But ah gets by. Don't need much, Ole Andy don't, and ain't none keen on company coming to call. So ah just sets here, watching de swamp critters such as yew, and knowing one fine morn ah won't be waking up. Ah sets here thinking back and knowing ah is satisfied wif what ah done wif my life."

"Don't yew miss all dem fancy cigars and sweet wine?" The turtle gazed at a scuffed and half-worn boot that rested haphazardly against the wall near the couch. "And dem all fine women wid de red lips and de big breasts?"

"Ah gots to admit sometimes Ole Andy, he misses dat stuff. But not de cigars or de wine, and shorely not dem fancy ladies." He snorted twice, large hurried gusts of air from his nose passing for laughter. "But I miss de power. De *power*, Doc, dat's all. Holding a man's life right here in de palm o' my hand, snuffing it out wif one snap o' my fingers." He paused for a moment of reflection, snapped his fingers loudly, and for the first time in perhaps years, a smile played at the corners of his lips. "Yessir, ah miss dat, ah shorely does."

The turtle continued his trek around the room, this time stopping to examine twenty or thirty fifty-dollar bills scattered on the floor near the table. Judging from the layer of dust on the bills it was not today or yesterday that the dust devil came skittering across the room, depositing the green paper about on the floor with no regard to its usefulness. The turtle knew Ole Andy had no need for money and wouldn't waste energy to get on his knees to pick it up.

"Don' yew worry dat de young bloods from town will come calling out here to yore shack? Dat deys come in here and rob yew?"

Doc asked. "Mabbe even kill yew and leave yer bones fer de swamp to take care of?"

Old Andy snorted his laughter again. "Dey's scared o' Ole Andy. Dey not be coming out here fer no reason."

"What makes de bloods scared of an ole man like yew?"

"Dey thinking dat Ole Andy, he might be turning dem into spiders er frogs er some udder little ole swamp critter. Dey knows it'll be dem what gets hurt, so dey keeps de distance. Good thing too, cos ah still gots tricks up de ole raggedy sleeves. Enough to handle a few bloods if dey gets froggy enough to hop ovah here."

"Well, dat's good," the turtle said. "No call fer younguns to treat ole peoples dat rough."

"Yessir, ah reckon." Andy eased his bare foot out in front of the turtle, stopping his forward movement. "What yew want, Doc? What yew want wif Ole Andy?"

Doc paused, then looked into the face of the Man. "Ah've come to tell yew very distinct dat it's time fer yew to be going home."

Ole Andy looked at Doc for a moment. He stared out through the open door, and saw in his mind a time and place distant from the swamp shack.

Summer: 1975

Uniformed in uncreased trousers and a blouse complete with the Victoria Cross, the self-proclaimed Field Marshall determined he would now be President for Life.

He issued a proclamation to the people and sat on his throne. He nodded and waved as he was borne up and carried through the city by the people he would govern. Men bowed. Women cast flowers as he passed. He snapped his fingers at a person, and the nearest soldier drew a bayonet and stabbed the person to death.

He snapped his fingers often.

4 July 1976.

Gunfire, commandos, a rescue of passengers from a commercial jet forced to land in Entebbe. Israeli hostages freed.

As for the President for Life …

He was extremely upset. How dare foreigners come into his country? This was *his* business, and he was more than capable of taking care of it! Fifty-eight minutes after the raid's onset, the plane was gone. Only two dead, and a grandmother left behind. The President for Life railed against any suspect, including 200 highly placed officials and the grandmother from the plane.

The President for Life walked onto a balcony above the plaza where they were herded.

"Let this be a lesson," he intoned. "No one collaborates with a raiding party of outsiders to make a mockery of my government, without paying a price. History bears witness to how I deal with rebellion."

He pointed to the Captain of the Guard and snapped his fingers. Cries, overcome by roars of many guns. As the President regarded the carnage, something nudged his foot. It was a saucer-sized turtle, so out of place and yet so familiar.

"Going home, am ah?" Andy said. "I knowed yew was no ordinary turtle." He released the bottle of moonshine. It clattered to the weatherboard floor and, because the floor was slanted, rolled until it hit a foot of the sideboard. "Yew say it's time Ole Andy be going home. Do yew mean back across de water, er do yew mean home as in Andy ain't gone be on dis ole mud ball no more?"

"Ah think yew knows de answer to dat, Andy. But lemme assure yew some ocean is gonna git crossed. By yew and me both, all right."

"Well, sir. I'm ready, I reckon. Gots a few things to do first, tidy up a bit, but that won't take long. No, sir, not long."

"What yew gots to do, Andy?" Doc said. "Ain't like yew gots de big fambily to say goodbye to, yew ate 'em."

"Reckon yer right about dat speculation, Doc. Ah ates dem. If yew had donkey-brained women and chillum like mine, yew would have ated dem. But ah does has one person ah gots to make peace wif, if dat's all right wif yew."

"Ah ain't got nothing but time, Ole Andy. Doc's got nothing but time. Jus' wondering as to who yew gonna try and get to forgive yew? God ain't in no mood fer it, yew done turned yer back on him mighty big. Took liberties wif his word."

"Don't yew reckon as to how God would forgive ole Andy if ah asked him real nice? Seems ah recall reading in de book how he would."

"Dat's in de book, shore enough," Doc said. "But yew done took too many eyes fer eyes, too many bites o' dat forbidden fruit, too many snaps o' yer fingers. Ain't no God gone overlook dat."

Andy shook his head. "Reckon yer right, Doc Green Turtle, but it don't matter none noways. Ain't God ah be wanting to talk to. Can be no peace tween de two o' us, cause don't neither o' us want it."

"Den who yew needing to be confessing to?"

"Ain't got but one person to talk to. Ah gots to try and find a way to tell myself goodbye."

"Get on wif it den."

Andy mumbled to himself for the better part of half an hour. Sometimes he went silent, sometimes he cried out loud. Sometimes he laughed, and now and again he shed tears, but in the end none of it mattered.

Together, they moved to the center of the room.

Doc swayed his head.

Before Andy's astonishment could turn to alarm, a gust of wind beat his face, squeezed new tears from his eyes. His life danced before him. Milton Obote, conqueror of Sir Edward Mutesa, slipped into a field of maize, his fallen government at his tail, as rebel troops sealed off Entebbe. Curfew, courts martial, examples made of traitors: live burials; village guillotines; boiling oil; crocs in the Tana River. Beggars, Indians, dissenters—all traitors—as much as Julius Kambarage Nyerere and his Tanzanians!

Andy saw Israeli hostages (oh, such joy!), then their rescue (rats!). He saw thirty mistresses, twenty children, one by one eaten to bone. He saw national debt, accusation, paranoia! Nyerere, the skunk! Libya, Jeddah, edge of the Great Swamp, USA.

Doc swayed his head even more. His eyes turned keen, hypnotic.

The Man tumbled to the floor, clutched his neck. He couldn't breathe, breathe, breathe!

Doc stilled his swaying.

The wind died.

The Man still lay on the floor, not in bedraggled garments and thongs made of old tire, but in paraphernalia, his old former royal self. His boots were buffed to a high polish. The medals on his breast shone like stars.

He rose, tested his heels, then stamped out a drill. He was ready to inspect the troops. He straightened, snapped his feet, lifted a hand to a salute.

Poised, he and Doc stepped out the door into a swirl of wind.

They flapped from a hurricane, crashed into a moonlit field full of golden maize. The Man regarded the rolling hills of corn and wondered if the East African Rail and the fifty-story buildings of his reign had thrived. He refused to help Doc Turtle from his backside, from his feet-up landing, and watched him rock himself to position.

They searched for the Royal City, through Jinja, Entebbe, all the way to Kampala. The Man was unable to swallow disbelief at the New Luganda and its immaculate cities, whitewashed and sparkling or bejeweled in marble and white gold. Instead of cars on the roads, air shuttles of stainless steel, double-glazed glass or platinum whistled overhead. He searched for a hint of squalor, of corruption, of street dogs, of vagrant beggars, and found none. Instead there was order, Medtronic centers, Braille libraries, spinal tap clinics, even Family First clinics and health spas. The New Luganda was not a country at war. Its buildings spiraled to the sky and glinted like diamonds. One building of pure glass and windows of crystal was shaped like the wings of a butterfly. Citizens fearless of the new soldier and his turtle simply wondered and were amused. They called him Soldier Turtle.

A peasant at the edge of the city stopped processing millet using an automatic grinder outside her hut that resembled a tree with branches made of shiny green material that blinked in strobe lighting. The Man nearly fell in astonishment. She cared to break cake with him (frosty-iced *cake,* not bread!), no recognition in her eyes. The Man broke into tears. Didn't she know who he was? he asked.

She shook her head.

The Man and Doc walked past children in a marble-glazed football field, progenies who were *not* learning the art of connecting a foot to an elusive ball but dang! were practicing a new brand of dance the Man had never seen. The music to which their bodies shimmied like bonefree puppets did not have songs in sweet Kakwa, his mother tongue; this music *zhinged!* and *zhanged!* and gave him a headache.

At the emerald lake, the Man and Doc beheld the Victoria. It was not murky like the bayou turned to bog outside the hut they had left behind. The waters were not infested with crocs that once lunged at prisoners condemned to death.

At the pink diamond palace, the Man demanded audience with the leader. Guards gazed at his regalia, at the turtle on his shoulder, and were so amused their eyes watered.

"Ah demand to see Milton, dat scoundrel, real dawg. Danged polecat stoles my country, plucked it under my foots. Ah darned well wants my nation back!"

Someone pointed out that Milton Obote was no longer in power; it was Emperor Museveni now. And they heckled him, turtle and all, away from the palace.

The Man roamed the streets of New Luganda. He told anyone who listened, the people of Luganda, that he was the Man, the *real Man* not an imposter. Some laughed and slapped him on his back; others pelted him with tomatoes. He lost Doc Turtle god-knows-where, and very nearly lost his mind.

One day, forlorn and hungry, he saw the diamond-crusted Regal Shuttle, a Diner plane, all glazed and blinking, on a slow glide overhead. It was the Emperor's shuttle. Sapphire head and taillights indicated a foreign visitor of import. The Man caught a glimpse of a silver-haired Nyerere, the nitwit, that dawg who had deposed him. President Nyerere sat beside Emperor Museveni.

What first was a glance out the window, the bedraggled man on the streets understood, became a flutter of recognition, then Nyerere turned away. The Man recalled the dishonor of years ago, moments before his ousting from power, when Nyerere's troops goaded the Man with Swahili songs of apocalypse:

Alikiona kizimba cha moto! / He saw a blast of fire!

Kilichomtoa nyoka pangoni mwake! / That scuttled the snake from his den!

As the shuttle rocketed into the horizon, Nyerere held something up against the gleaming window before the shuttle vanished into the sun. It was Doc Green Turtle, dang scoundrel, now sojourning with the Emperor and his guests.

The Man stared until there was no more to see.

The song of apocalypse grew loud, louder in his ears:

Nyoka pangoni mwake! / The snake from his den!

Alikiona kizimba cha moto! / He saw a blast of fire!

As he tramped the streets, the loudness in his ears became unbearable. He crouched, put hands to his head and rocked until the singing silenced. He gathered empty tins of Cowboy ghee, discarded and futureless, clanked them and heard no sound. So he tied them to his ankles. The Man faced the sun, shielded his eyes from its fire, and set one foot before the other in a slow march to eternal anonymity.

A TASTE OF UNGUJA

NOT JUST ANY son, he's *the* son. The one, the only. He loves fresh banana bread with a drizzle of maple syrup. Now you've lost him.

The loss in your heart is desert dry. Your pulse is fast, loud in your ears. You languish in the scent of the impossible: how you carried something in your body a whole nine months, then misplaced it. Not by choice, taken. Because when love sours, emotion is bare. That Z, if he could … he has. Taken your son.

You sit with a rock on your lap, not a metaphoric rock. It's a real rock, the size of Z's head. You lifted it from the botanical gardens where it guarded a new flowerbed. Z's name is written on every jagged facet of this stone—you chose it precisely for him, saw the scatter of brain matter on the rock, the smashing soon-to-be. An ooze of white, or cream. A porridge of tissue, a spurt of blood.

There's a girl in a bodysuit facing you two seats up in the tram. You wonder if—behind the mask—she's frowning. She looks at the rock, but you don't care. Time is a tricky memory, more so when masks float about. Most of them, like yours, are cheap disposables, pale blue outside, white inside. But there are people who manoeuvre the world with bandanas on their noses. There's a boy with a red cap. His mask is dusky. He's wrapped in a puffed-out jacket against the night cold. Then you see his eyes and realize it's not a boy but a grown Asian woman. There's a teen with a luminescent mask. A sheaf of curls on her head runs with the breeze through the slit of the tram window. Wind that starts anywhere, ends here.

The tram is not a roomy one. Is there enough social distance between you and the other passengers? You distract yourself with colors. The tram is an ancient thing, green and white. Each yellow door has a red sign that says STOP. Its black face up the front, all glass. Its gloomy crown with a feeler, a tentacle reaching for the sky. The driver and their hi-vis, a screaming orange. The tram squeals and hums, groans, wobbles, rolls and jerks. *Ting!* It's off to the next stop, closer to your deed, where you'll follow your feet and wait in the dark.

When Z took your son, you felt hot and cold. But the system didn't care how you felt. The system said Z did what he could. It said you were an 'other', your intentions unclear. Z was from here, a color the system knew. It trusted him, not you, with the safety of your son. You could hear their reasoning: *What's to stop you from stealing him, somewhere remote to the Sahara—where would we find the little one in that weird heat? Or Lake Victoria, islands everywhere—what's to stop you from hiding him in a crocodile? Or Mount Kilimanjaro, the tallest point in Africa—5895 meters and then some. You could bury him in a glacier, we'd never know where to start.* They didn't care you were from none of those places.

A court order said you couldn't be within 100 meters of your son. Someone called an ambulance for your collapse, but it was a hole in your heart no medicine could restore. You were alone, no one to help in your greatest need. Z's action—a man denying a woman her own child—was an apocalypse. It violated your culture: a child belongs to his mother.

Ting! You step off the tram.

You stand there with your stone, you don't know how long. The sky bellows, it begins to rain. You still feel them together: heat and cold. A month of heat wrapped in a moment. An ice-covered mist submerging the essence of you until you're drowning.

Drowning.

You'd rather see the sun, even when its whiteness shimmers to blackness.

Tonight's rain is an unfurling of pins, twirling towards you in the shape of a cloak. Their pricks numb you from flying branches and debris succumbing to the deluge. You see the remains of a book, bushed and damp at your boots.

There's a nightjar. You wonder about it, calling, soft churring notes. It flaps slow wings in the rain, a beat that's almost hypnotic. Long wings you feel drawn to. A nightjar is the totem of your clan. And when it lands feet away, yours is a deep connection with the shine of its rubied eye. You draw near until you touch the bird, until the wet of its feathers turns to gold, black and brown. But there's rain, more rain. You wish for the sun.

You remember the caesarean, the soft pull almost a tickle, an epidural dulling your spine. He came out clean—how quickly they wiped him—eager for a tit. Three years on, he roared out his fear, but you held him. As the nurse pushed in a needle, you gripped the boy and your heart cracked over. You held him like a vax was life and death, because it was.

When Z took him to Mount Martha—a boys' weekend with the cousins—it was the first time you'd parted from the child for more than a day. You went near mad with longing but couldn't reach your son on Z's smart phone, the signal so bad there. And finally, when the phone rang on that end, Z answered and put your son on.

The boy said, "Mama." Your heart stopped beating. "What shall I do for food?" And you died.

Died.

When your heart came back, and breath floated in, you asked, "What about your father?"

And your son said, "He doesn't know."

Again you died.

So you drove all the way to Woolworths, swiped shelves into a trolley. The man at the checkout looked at you like you were nuts. A hoarder: Pasta. Pasta sauce. Chocolate. Iced tea. Vegetables and steak.

Sausages. Chicken. Packs and packs of two-minute noodles. Lots of milk. A clutch of canned tuna. The supplies all fit in the car, though the boot nearly didn't close. You drove an hour and five minutes all the way through the M1 on the EastLink, the M3 and Mornington Peninsula Freeway, the M11 to Moorooduc Highway, the exit 19 to Mount Martha, because that's what …

A mother does.

In a confusing arena of sin and struggle, pedophiles in masks demand protection as marginalized persons with an attraction to little people. Their expressions are fresh as snow, in a bible's name. They speak in a way that uses the creative process of a serpent to bring definition, no punctuation, to the term "freedom" and all shorthand modes that take or give, and dance with thunder. What's your confession, oh flesh and blood? We may eat of the fruits of the garden, they say, fingers on their hearts. Story after story their words morph in shifts and changes, but each subject and predicate, noun, verb or adjective is a weapon of mass destruction complete with apathy. Nowhere is their weakness more dramatic than in each war of words. You think about this, standing in the rain. But Z is not a pedophile, and you're not sure it's a good thing. His act towards you is monstrous.

There's no monster inside.

Yellow-lidded bins—it's collection night.

Love is not part of what you lost; you can't lose what you never had. Love never was. For your son, yes. For Z, no. How do you love someone empty?

Maybe it wasn't Z who was empty.

He's a creature of habit, is Z, that's how you'll get him. Tonight, it's yellow bins.

You stand outside his gate with your rock. It doesn't matter that curfew is looming—before long he'll wheel out the bin.

But the nightjar is calling, calling, soft churring notes, flapping, flapping in the rain. *Life is a bee,* sings a melody in your head to the nightjar's. *And a bee leaves a stinger inside you.* Something about the tune …

You drop the stone in a trance, follow the nightjar's singing. *Unlike the bee, life doesn't die. It never does, only you.* A discarded mail-van by a girl's school. Suddenly you're walking up a hill and it says Clowes Street. *Stay safe, stay well,* a sign says. Red-brick houses with ebony windowsills, shadowy garage doors. gray posh houses with ivy climbing up walls, grilled gates. Manicured hedges a rich olive. Flats. Units. But the world is moving like a jigsaw, everything shifting.

There's a grandfather tree. What happened to Z's suburb, immobile cars lining its street, the ghosts of pay stations? Now you're in a botanical garden, not the one that gave you the rock. A low-flying plane rumbles overhead. Then you see it: *313 The Gateway,* next to an underground car park. Your sanity jars. How's this possible in the middle of a garden? Your feet push another inch. Without warning you slip down a track, a noiseless fall. You sit up, bushed. The night is a rubbish tip. You've lost your face mask.

There's the nightjar beckoning you to follow and, like a fool, you do. You push past a sign that says: *No entry.*

Safe is the old limit, not a delta into the evening. *A Taste of Unguja,* says a blinking neon you've never seen before. Another sign says: *We're open.*

Karibu sana, a wooden placard with its welcome, crooked on the entry before you step into the building's arcade, and into the soul of Zanzibar. Sweet taarab music seeps gently into your space. It's music so full of want, you notice details in its notes: the vibrato and staccato of an accordion. The sweet wail of a reed flute. The rhythm of clapsticks. A hollow *click, click* in the claves. A fall of pebbles in the rattle and shake of the maracas. Lyrics full of poetry, adages and proverbs in a repeated phrase whose modulation is a funereal jazz eddying spice, ripples and scales.

The walls have silhouettes of dhows and wild cats. A cheetah cocks its head in the savannah, scanning the horizon as if listening for something. It rises in a crouch, disappears in the grasslands. But you can tell from the sway of grass that the beast is stalking towards you. It bursts from the scrub in a sprint, nimble lopes in a shadow. You are the kill.

You stand rooted, helpless in fascination more than fear. You smell the cheetah's wet fur from its sweat, the rot in her breath as a paw lifts in speed to knock you down …

"Table for one?"

The voice startles you. The waiter has one leg, the other is a spade. His eyes are a sound, a howl that spills. His name is embossed on the breast of a ghost-white shirt: *Nungui.*

"What?" you say absently, as your eyes return to the cheetah, head cocked in pose in a painting on the wall.

"I asked if you needed a table for one." Nungui's voice comes and goes.

But, finally, you can relax—yes, a table for one.

There's something about the compilation of the restaurant, so hidden you fell into it. You wonder why it's open long after curfew inside a metropolis in a state of disaster. You look at the nothingness all about. Steamed-up windows yet broken. So cool inside, it's freezing. Like a spare bedroom in a winter cabin. Is that a black cat on the windowsill? And a red lizard? The place smells of lilacs and toilet freshener, the fake politeness of a wake. The walls, the chairs are shining, everything polished like a coffin. A trio of slit-eyed goats nibble at a curtain, right there near that table.

The menu is a party scene that ends in tears—why did you think that?

You place your order of potluck full of spice: cumin, turmeric, paprika and cloves. "Mchuzi wa pweza," you say, mindless that your own voice is a sound falling, a clatter of pebble, a lone one, down a staircase.

"Octopus curry," says Nungui. "Fresh from a coral rock, best in the house."

He offers you a cocktail from a tray. You see the sun in the flute of tamarind, a sticky syrup, sweet and sour. You chew on the pulp that strangely tastes of coconut, before it sours.

Nungui appears as if in a blink. He holds in bare hands a steaming clay pot. Are those frogs and tea leaves? You're dissolving, the desert on your tongue. Nungui's plucked-off fingers rest on your table. Removed from his body, holding a plate of your lifetime, not many years left to run. You wonder if he knows that his leg is a spade. His skin is flaking, his muscles falling.

You fear for a moment that the fingers will climb into your chowder. But they skitter back to his now skeletal frame. You lift a spoon to your mouth. The chowder is a lumpy thing that tastes of hopelessness and despondency, a bird with broken wings, an elephant graveyard, a dead baby, stepping on a landmine, a slow erosion of the body by cancer. Your mood plummets with every mouthful.

"Don't you like it?" Nungui's voice is a nonvoice. His face is gone —in its place teeth and bone. A dent where eyes should be. The music is playing over and over. It's full of scales in your head. Your heart drops beneath the table.

You hear them before you see them. A murmur of sound. A fragment of senseless words and phrases floating above your head: *Pulpits. Cards. Horseshoes. Is that a flood or a fire? It's a bleed of basements, pools and spools filled with scratches and howls.*

You see them at a table together, near where the goats were. They're not looking at you. They're the only patrons beside you. Dead people, their eyes full of tar. But they're not just people or dead. They're *your dead people.*

There's your grandfather, ash-hair, wisdom eyes, half his body unclothed. A pale sarong made of batik is tied around his waist. He died of hopelessness. There's your grandmother, tiny, sweet-faced, her spine all bent. She's wearing a chitenge sprigged with sunflowers. She died of heartbreak. There's your mother, kind-lipped, the eyes of a fawn. She died early, killed her own mother with heartbreak. There's your father. A thousand suns in his smile. He's wearing a breasted safari suit the color of the Sahara. He died of heart, liver and kidney disease. There's your sister, isn't she the picture? Tiny nose, fair skin, elastic hair falling to her knees. She died of anguish—there's the son she lost, the other son, the daughter just a bub.

You wonder if they're the same as you knew them. Your family. You fear you'll never know the answer. Your own son's face, once imprinted in memory, is now an unknowing. You can't bring yourself to look at a photograph, his photo, the apocalypse too devastating, each fading memory a fresh atomic bomb that disintegrates you anew.

They're playing a card game with the intensity of a fisherperson casting a net. But it's all reverse—it's the baby who's the dealer, shuffling, reshuffling the decks of cards, her hole card facedown as the others stand or hit. Everything is backward, even Nungui. He's facing wrong, a sly grin cast your way. You wonder at his posterior, his hands, the skeletal foot of his good leg ... directed away from you.

The taarab music with its dhows and waves is loud, louder. Your grandfather stands, swaying to its tune. He loosens the batik wrapped around his waist, lets it fall. He turns, bends his knees and bares his buttocks. Your grandmother stands. She unknots the chitenge from the shoulders. It falls to her feet. Paper breasts, a gnarl of skin. She has no underclothing. She turns, bares her behind. Your father unbuttons, then unzips the khaki trousers of his safari suit. He peels it down his legs, steps out of his underwear. He turns ... Your mother lifts her batik ... It's a procession, an orchestra of motion. Silent music as your sister lifts her sunflower dress, pulls down her panties and bares her bottom.

It goes on, until the baby undoes the lilac- and pink-headed pins of her white nappy the texture of a towel. It's soiled. A smell of bad fish, dead rat hits you. She bends, bares her bottom. Only then do you cry out, a sound whose vehemence climbs from your stomach, falls out of your throat, and you're gagging. The expulsion is twisting, jolting. You convulse to the floor, your mouth foaming, failing in its pleas to your family that they don't, please stop. Because you know, yes you know, how a curse is summoned.

Oblivious to your appeal—the music now loudest in your head, a melody with the roar of oceans—your relatives begin a synchrony of dance. It abruptly stops with a throttle of the flute. The funereal wail of the Swahili jazz is gone. Your people straighten, reclothe, one by one. Now they look at you in silence.

The nightjar is flapping, beating at your face with his wings. He calls you, calls you, soft churring notes. He flies towards the exit, then back. Calling, soft churring notes.

He wants you to follow.

You climb to your feet, turn one last time to speak to your family, but see only three slit-eyed goats nibbling at a curtain. Your head is woozy. Nungui is whole again, the name tag on his ghost-white shirt. Your smile to him is an apology, the haste in your leaving.

"How much?" you manage to say.

"The Gateway," he says. "On the house."

You pass the cheetah, running backward in slow motion, a silhouette receding from your view. You hear Nungui's words behind you, in front of you, everywhere, as you stumble, fall out of the void and into the air of smoke at dawn: "You're welcome."

Karibu tena, the placard's invitation now different, still crooked on your way out of the building's arcade. You doubt very much that you'll be coming back. Somewhere in your mind you know that if you came back tomorrow, you'd find nothing of tonight here. Suddenly, you get it. The message your dead were giving. You're not alone but cocooned in tradition, from one side of the world to the other.

Two coppers stop you. "Out and about? At this time?"

You blink.

"There's a pandemic. Ten minutes earlier, it would have been a fine. But we get it, curfew is over."

"Over?"

"It's 5.10 am, mate. What you need is a mask."

They hand you one, the cheap disposable one—pale blue outside, white inside.

Your legs are strings. You follow the nightjar down the hill. The world moves in puzzle, everything morphing. Before long you'll reach Z's suburb, cars lining the street. Your rock is waiting for him to collect his bin. You have the rage to do it.

When he appears, you'll step into the light. He'll soften at the sight of you, sorry for what he's done. He'll think you've come to beg back into his life, even as he says, "The fuck are you doing here?"

Wasn't the separation your idea? It was meant to be temporary, something a marriage counsellor could fix. You just needed room to sort out your head, to face your fate in the grind of a loveless marriage. You never loved. It was Z who was enamored by you. The sight of you now will again swing the axe of his loss, the one that spilled cruelty out of him. There's no salve for it. Some bridges you eternally scorch, and that's that. He took matters to an unspeakable place.

You won't say, "Screw you, Z," the words you've thought over and over since that fateful day he took your son and filed an injunction. You cried narrow lanes and carved doors. You cried dhows. You cried to the Indian Ocean and to Mother Africa. The time for "Screw you, Z" is past. Instead, you'll walk on asphalt into the light, as a keening wail of taarab music fills your head. You'll spin and give Z your backside. You'll hear yourself say in a voice inside a voice, "You should see this."

The melody whirling in your head will be a sweet seduction, the croon of a violin pining for islands. There'll be nothing sexual or seductive about the ritual. You'll lift your skirt to the bass drone of drums. Pull your knickers to bare your black bottom, and sway, sway to the airy tootle of a flute, as the nightjar churrs, flapping overhead—the totem of your ancestors.

What Z will get is a taste of Unguja. You'll seal his fate to where no one, not even you, can undo it. Because what you have is the gift of a curse. You'll get your son back. You'll give him fresh banana bread with a drizzle of maple syrup.

As for your cursed ex ... He'll set roaming, roaming, homeless on the streets of Melbourne. Nothing can save him.

FORGETTING TOOLERN

SOYA WAS SITTING and minding her own business at HM-Harrods and its floating gardens, cushioned in its seats like billows of cloud, when a wild-eyed Englishman with runaway hair and pointing a buzzing device threw himself at her.

She knew at once that chivalry was dead.

"Toolern," he said with excitement. "And you're not from around here."

"To Learn?"

"That's right. And this —" He nodded at the squealing device. "It's my alien detector. You've just set it off. What's a scrumptious dark chocolate like you doing in a colorless place like this?"

"What if I don't answer your question?"

He pressed the handle, and the darned thing stopped squealing. "I'll just ask it differently. New in this part of the world?"

"Not so much."

"What brings you to New London?"

Soya wore her coy smile. "I hear the city has some fine male specimens."

He pushed his face even closer to hers, his smile bigger. "You're looking at one."

"They just need to do you up a bit."

He stared at her for a long time. "Do what?"

"Your face. Your hair."

He laughed. "Never. I like how I come."

"A New Londoner." She considered his owl face. "Are you available?"

"Technically, I'm not from here," he said. "But I'm always available. Would you like to see my spacer?"

"Your what?"

He grabbed her arm, "Come," before she could protest. He guided the pillow float to the exit, gave the waiter in a coat with tails a generous tip, and bounced Soya out into the street where he pointed at an abandoned ice-cream van.

It was full of controls. She moved to touch a handle.

"Don't!" His bark startled her. "I wouldn't touch that. Unless you want to find yourself in Gliese, Super Saturn or the Waterworld. But you're welcome to this." He slapped a wall, and a fully furnished king bed fell from it. "Would you like a shag?"

"What?!"

"Emma's seeking an audience with the queen —"

"Who's Emma and what's she got to do with whether or not I want a sh—seriously!"

"Emma's my travel assistant, and we need to convince the queen to part with her crown, only for a moment, to appease the ghosts of desires, otherwise the Cancriens will obliterate the entire universe."

That's how it all started. And some consummation did happen, very eventfully, because Toolern knew exactly how to give a woman pleasure.

The "assistant" Emma arrived without warning, a twinkling coronet in her hand. Blood lips and high cheekbones—she was a flowing-haired stunner, as beautiful as a planet on her own, breathtaking with the coronet and a stern face. Soya was certain she'd turn lesbian in a blink for this Emma.

"That's not a crown," said Toolern.

"This is all you get," Emma said to him, never mind he was naked-arsed with a woman beneath him. "It would be very nice if you could thank me for trying."

Soya appeared the only one uncomfortable in the situation.

"We have a universe to save," said Toolern and pushed her out of the spacer as she was putting on her boots.

Emma was already fiddling with the controls Toolern had

forbidden Soya from touching, and the spacer was beginning to rev and hump.

His visits to New London were frequent, and always from some wild expedition with his exotic assistant who seemed to neither like nor dislike Soya. Emma just wanted to get the job done, whichever job, and somehow Soya always felt in the way of it.

Toolern never visited Soya's apartment in St James's Park. He preferred to leave the spacer—that abandoned ice-cream van painted with overflowing waffle cones, pretzel cones and twin choc-dipped cones—across the street and bring her into it for some quick intimacy, during which time Emma managed to make herself scarce.

Toolern never asked questions of Soya, showed no curiosity about where she'd come from. Soya couldn't understand her own determined liking of Toolern. With this Englishman she was boiling the Thames. He was guarded roof to cellar. Miles of chasing, she was nowhere near his heart. He gave in fistfuls and segments, never in bucketloads. If she drew near, he loped, skittered and dived into the furthest planet. Took him entire days to soar back to New London with his revving spacer.

And he was a perfectionist; she suspected that he questioned if she was enough. That he was never looking for "the one". What was it with men, and their "assistants"? But right now, Toolern was a good problem to have, unlike some fruit loops she'd dated in the past. Her romance history across the universe, and centuries, was smeared with breaks, swirls, clatters and cracks. Occasionally there were gallops—his or hers. She'd hoped to find love in New London. But Toolern was a blackhole: strong enough to bend light, warped in his distorted space and time.

He would garble like a mad scientist about confetti planets, folding Aztecs, gone-away warlocks or instant oceans, but when it came to spicing up romance, he was almost passionless. Uncrackable his calm, even when she sent him a hologram of herself in lingerie. The indifference in this New Londoner who insisted he wasn't from this planet still stunned.

But his kiss, when he gave it, was poetic, an abundance of butterflies and honey. It dappled her soul with peach, ginger and lime. Think colors: corals. His caress was both virgin and capable, and she gasped and strained in his arms. It wasn't just sex. There was a kind of cosmic enchantment that swathed her in its glow the moment he laid a finger, tongue or toe on her skin. He didn't like feral talk and lost his erection the one time she showed him an exotic plug. With him it wasn't sex; it was a dance. An elegant dance.

During intimacy, he was present. His touch—lip, tongue, finger or toe—conducted an orchestra inside her body. It was that presence that made up for gaps in his self-created absences. How he guarded his independence! Sometimes Soya felt he treated his assistant better than he did her. He'd drop everything and sprint to Emma without a blink if she beckoned. As for Soya, she had to milk time.

Within days of agreeing to be "exclusive" Toolern announced an impromptu trip—it could take months or years, he explained. He was going to The Pulse of Planets with his Emma. Soya's jaw dropped. Before she could stammer, "What about us?" his words tumbled out: "Let's take a break. Until I'm back. I'm not sure I'll be wanting to continue."

He'd chosen to dine her in the spacer, his Emma fiddling with some controls and pretending not to listen ... Soya couldn't make a scene.

"Break?" she said it like a word whose meaning she didn't recognize.

Toolern moved slightly away, as if Soya's emotiveness overwhelmed him. But her look must have shaken out the explanation. He discharged a careful speech about an inability to commit to one person.

"You want a b-break? Like seeing other p-people?"

"That's not a factor. I'm going to save worlds. I won't have time for other women."

"A break." Air in her head. There was nothing optional about his proposal. "We won't even talk?"

"I'm happy to communicate. Let's hologram."

Later, much later, she remembered a dog just outside the spacer: the beast yowled when her heels clipped its tail. A low-flying spacer: it soared above her head as she stumbled to near suicide from eyes blinded with tears. She remembered the air, filled with a stench of dead corals. She didn't remember how she got home to St James's Park.

A break until he got back?

Would have been nice if he'd shared his fear of commitment before he slapped down the bed and nudged her to their first intimacy. She pondered whether to snip the head off whatever it was they had. She wrestled with the thought a couple of days. Finally sent him a hologram:

You've managed to hurl a grenade at a fine working relationship. Your kind, you will never run out of grenades.

It unharnessed a response: *What do you mean "your kind"?*

She replied: *Chronic relationship killers.*

He replied: *Sounds like supervillain megaslayers—the way you put it. Shall we talk?*

She met him outside the spacer. She towered him in her heels. But one kiss straight from a wild bees' honeycomb, and her sophistication collapsed. She forgot everything, forgave massacre.

Alas, back in her apartment, bewilderment returned. But his new holo, all it said was, *hey*, lifted her to rhapsody. She was in love, she realized, madly, madly.

Just before dawn, her holo came alive and it was Toolern. "It's me," he said, as if she couldn't tell. What she could certainly tell were the sounds of Emma operating controls, the spacer honking like a mule and ready to transverse into space.

She waited for the inevitable break-up, then it dawned, seconds into the holo: he only wanted to connect.

"I think," she said hesitantly, "we have a good synergy together. How about we see how we go?"

"I agree," he said.

Good. No more rubbish of breaks.

She grew morose as days passed, but she put it down to January blues. She missed the bark of his laughter, the peer in his mad-scientist gaze. His owl face and ridiculous hair. Sensual lips that delivered the sweetest kiss full of honey and butterflies.

Her spirits lifted when she woke to a holographic avatar, and there was her Toolern smiling at her in cool English charm.

She was content to impartial holos two or three days after her own earnest holos. He sent her a recreation of his battle with the People of Flesh and Gold, how he destroyed the brain of the Superclown, a whole mutant clan with it. Then there was a canoe-rafting holo in a white river wash, the image bright with Toolern's jungle smile and Emma's raw glee as she fell into him, flowing hair whipping his face, on some remote planet.

Soya's holo said: *Promise you'll take me on an adventure? When are you back?*

One day, three seconds. Silence.

X

Two days, five hours, twenty-one seconds. Silence.

Xx

Three days, eleven hours, forty-two seconds.

Still silence.

By the fourth day, her bile was spilling.

She sent another holo: *Need that much thinking? XX*

It whisked out a response: *We've been in battle! The Pink Planet versus hat-P-7b—did I tell you it rains rubies and sapphires there? The Pinkers need me, but I'm not a god for them. And I'm not a god for you either!*

It appeared she'd stirred Mr Passionless, pulled his anger out alive.

She sat on his response a whole day. Awoke to his second holo at dawn: *Sometimes your messages make me uneasy.*

Exhilaration, he was sharing feelings.

Now she responded: *I guess, every now and then, I just need reassurance. x*

He sat on it a whole day. And then his holo arrived. It was 3 a.m. her time, he'd woken her up to tell her this. All she saw was a bunch of dancing images. He was someplace remote, the lip-sync off. But the message that arrived seconds after his lips moved walloped home: *Reassurance is something I cannot give. I agreed to stay in communication.*

Soya fell back a moment. She'd clung to a hope that the situation was only passing. That they would construct their relationship when he came back to New London. His words confirmed there were no bones to salvage: the vacillation was a forever thing.

Inside, she erupted. Her anger surged from her stomach to her throat. She wanted to unleash a scream that spiraled upwards and outwards. What man was this?

Outside, to him, not a word. Her way of punishing him. After weeks of his unnoticing her silence, she determined that she *just wouldn't* anymore. Wait for him to come round, now or whenever.

She installed a firewall to his holograms. The action *communicated* her entire feelings, or a darn good approximation of them. After the swirl of him, this crack was hers, of her doing, a fatal gorge. She was happy to own it. She was done with men who threw her bones. Plummeted any such man to where he could never destroy her.

She went to an upside-down aquatic center just off Waterloo Road and in walking distance to the war museum. She dived up into the water and swam like a whale was blowing the pool. Lap after lap, she mentally reconstructed his holos. Communication? Communication! She hated those words. Detached holos every third day, that was his idea of communication? What about the butterflies, the honey, the waltz? How he put a melt in her skin? What was that if it meant zilch?

She walked home under a brooding moon. Not that she missed Toolern. Right now, she couldn't bear to think of his face. Quite simply, her obsession—is that what it was?—had dissipated. His dazzle faded.

An avatar slipped up on her screen, and she latched onto it: Zed. A South Londoner. Months back she and Zed had gone on a couple of dates. They'd met on some hologram dating site. He spoke so badly, how was he even English? But he was. Born and bred in Croydon. Even though the Home Office and its bureaucracy had long since moved to virtual, and now provided robotic automation at its best, it left behind the old Croydon. The u-bend suburb was still quite beat yet compact, a shabby sort packed with rough patches and dodgy crowds. It was wholly starved of New London's theatre and fine-dining culture.

But Zed's holo profile said he liked fine dining, cafés, local pubs and art exhibitions. He travelled big, just never interstellar. Great circle of friends, a bit surprising for the self-deprecating sort he turned out to be. Perhaps bitter about women—he'd talked about a couple of bad experiences. Slogged the evening. Nothing came of those dates with him.

She holo'ed him now anyway. *Catch up for a drink?*

His holo was instant (unlike someone she knew): *Nawmally I would say yes. You'ave an advantage over me ... Know what I mean?*

Her holo: *N-no.*

His holo: *How've yew been? Yes, a drink. OK?*

Monday night he picked her up in his spacer. Brushed her lips lightly with his. He was as she remembered: tall, goodlooking-ish, ash-crop head. He took her to Michelin House, afloat like a giant eagle above Canary Wharf.

He remembered everything about her, things she'd told him those many months ago: how she swam daily, her passion for Rory King's *Liberate Your Imagination*, her favorite holo show: *The Mentalist*.

Unlike those first two dates when he was remote, listened with polite silence to her small talk—no wonder they had never eventuated to anything—in this one Zed was different. He was reborn: opening doors, fingering her waist, taking her hand across the table to such extent she needed talent to manoeuvre cutlery, slice her steak, sip her wine.

"Dated other people?" she asked.

"This woman, nuff said, yeah? Dog was 'er kid, it lived indoors. Slept in 'er bed. You turned ter give a cuddle, dog's brearf in yaaahr face. I set up a romantic getaway, got a luxury bouquet what came along wiv chocolates: presen'ed da voucher. *But da dog,* she said. *Can't go wivaaaht da dog*. Eight months ov da dog was mawer van enough, innit. And you?"

She started to tell him about Toolern, then shook her head. "Nothing unforgettable."

He laughed lightly at her jokes, asked questions about her likes, dislikes ... The gold in his pupils magnetized her.

"What do you like in a woman?" she asked.

"Lingerie. Heels. Lips. OK?"

"A bit shallow. But honest, I give you that."

A few things set off a siren or two, like he'd been wed twice. She didn't know that. "What happened?" she asked.

"Three fngs. I'll tell yew in 'er words." The way he said it, she didn't want to be on the other end of that curled lip. "Blimey! One she said I was controlling, planned all 'olidays. She never arranged anyfng, didn' know 'ow. And sure, I put me foot down when I 'ad a problem wiv a 'oliday in Hawaii five times in a row. Nuff said, yeah?"

"Two?"

"She said I was not thankful. Seriously laughable. Nuff said, yeah."

"What was the third thing?"

"This one I agree wiv. She said I was critical. If yew ask me opinion, I'll give it. If yew say, *Honey, is me ass all big in dis dress,* and it is, sorted, mate, I'll say it's all big. Why ask if yew don' wan' da truth?"

"And the second wife?"

"Dat was number two. De first, we married young. When I said I'm movin' out, she didn' protest. Know what I mean?"

But the gold in his eyes … And the restaurant: the lighting, the music, the smells, the choice of wine—she was heady.

He spoke lightly in the spacer. Touched her thigh when he shifted gears. A lemon moon on the horizon, the promise of a proper relationship … Her riotous heart. She did not hesitate to ask him in for coffee at St James's Park. He didn't refuse. She swooned in his arms the instant her front door opened, melted as he whispered, "Now it begins," against her lips. Moaned as his mouth swallowed hers.

He left quietly.

No hologram the following day, or the next. Nothing thanked her for a fabulous evening.

Finally, she broke her resolve, holo'ed: *Lingerie, heels and lips. You got all three. x*

His response was instant: *Runnin' late. Cheers. OK?*

Knocked her breath out a full minute.

When her lungs recovered, she weighed if Zed's was a gallop. Then she questioned if she was the problem. But how could she be? She was independent, not clingy or *that* knee-jerking. She'd endured dung. The godparent of dung. An entire clan and super clan of dung.

She wanted to reach a pillow and cry.

Toolern and his Emma were changing history in missions to the unknown. Visiting phantasmic worlds and rescuing women who fell to Earth—just not this woman. Here she was in New London, her heart cracking.

Just then a hologram trembled in her room. It was Zed.

Doubt, he said. *I always get it. Tend ter over fnk. How've yew been? OK?*

She stared at the message for a long time, and reminded herself she was done with men who threw her bones.

Resolute, she blocked Zed.

COLLABORATING AUTHORS

ANDREW HOOK is a European writer who has been published extensively in the independent press since 1994, with over 160 short stories in print. His seventh short story collection, *Frequencies of Existence,* was recently published by NewCon Press, and he can be found at www.andrew-hook.com.

SEB DOUBINSKY is a bilingual award-winning writer born in Paris. His novels, all set in a dystopian universe revolving around competing cities-states, have been published in the UK and in the USA. He currently lives with his family in Aarhus, Denmark, where he teaches at the university.

E. DON HARPE has had a varied career, from military service in the 1960s to industrial engineering. He is a published Nashville songwriter and a real descendant of the Harpe Brothers, America's first serial killers. Harpe has nearly forty short stories, including two in the *Twisted Tales II* anthology that won the Eppie Award for best science fiction anthology in 2007. Now retired and living in North Georgia, Harpe devotes his time to his family and to his writing.

ABOUT THE AUTHOR

EUGEN BACON is an African Australian author of several novels and fiction collections. She's a finalist in the 2022 World Fantasy Award. Eugen was announced in the honor list of the 2022 Otherwise Fellowships for 'doing exciting work in gender and speculative fiction'. Her short story collection Danged Black Thing made the 2021 Otherwise Honor List. Eugen has won, been longlisted or commended in international awards, including the Aurealis Award, Foreword Indies, Bridport Prize, Copyright Agency Prize, Horror Writers Association Diversity Grant, Otherwise, Rhysling, Elgin, Australian Shadows, Ditmar Awards and Nommo Awards for Speculative Fiction by Africans.

Visit her website at eugenbacon.com and Twitter feed @EugenBacon

ALSO BY EUGEN BACON

FICTION

Broken Paradise

Chasing Whispers

Mage of Fools

Saving Shadows

Danged Black Thing

Speculate (with Dominique Hecq)

The Road to Woop Woop & Other Stories

Ivory's Story

Black Moon: Graphic Speculative Flash Fiction

Hadithi & The State of Black Speculative Fiction (with Milton Davis)

It's Folking Political

Her Bitch Dress

Claiming T-Mo

NON-FICTION

An Earnest Blackness

Writing Speculative Fiction

ZEN THE ART
OF
STARSHIP
MAINTENANCE
AND OTHER STORIES
TOBIAS S BUCKELL

CPSIA information can be obtained
at www.ICGtesting.com
Printed in the USA
JSHW012333240523
42219JS00002B/14

9 781955 765114